MAKING FRIENDS

BACK TO THE DRAWING BOARD

KRISTEN GUDSNUK

MAKiNG

BACK TO THE DRAWING

graphix
An Imprint of
SCHOLASTIC

FRiENDS
BOARD

Library of Congress Control Number: 2019932098

ISBN 978-1-338-13927-3 (hardcover)
ISBN 978-1-338-13926-6 (paperback)

10 9 8 7 6 5 4 3 2 1 19 20 21 22 23

Printed in China 62
First edition, August 2019
Edited by Adam Rau
Book design by Phil Falco
Publisher: David Saylor

To Kathryn.

Splintered Dreams of MAGIC
The Danielle Radley Story
BY DANIELLE RADLEY
A DANYRAD PRODUCTION™
magical
WOW!
CAST!
Joan Quincy and Leah Tung:
HUGZ!!
Childhood Friends 5-ever!
Joan
Leah
•Friend unit (not sold separately)
•Not in my classes anymore
•They have abandoned me
Tom Torres:
...He's pretty cool.
•in some of my classes
•boy
•???
a book?!
MAGE PROPHECY RVNE QUEST walkthrough
Nick Maloney:
Still a jerk.
•my nemesis
•no redeeming qualities
•briefly an actual pig
THE WORST
Madison Fontaine:
I'm churlish!?
Too cool for school, but here she is anyway.
•Churleader
•magical
•bff
•Foster Kid
Aleesha Robinson:
She's writing an oboe concierto. What are YOU doing with your life?
A+
•THE Kid to cheat off in any class
•Solar Sister!
Cara McCoy:
It must be nice to be her.
•Madison and Aleesha's friend (not mine)
•Mysterious
•Rude Fine
•popularity Final Boss
Lauren Radley:
my big Siste
FSSSS!
SHUT UP UR ANNOYING
I'm stoopid
Linda and Chuck Radley:
•my parents
•They won the Cash4Lyfe lotto!
•Otherwise boring people
C4L
Linda + Chuck
$2,000/WEEK
$2000
Lotto
...and ME!
Danielle Radley.
But my friends call me Dany.
magically long hair (Thanks, Prince Neptune!)
Fix later
y-you remember me, right??
•possessor of unimaginable power
•7th grader
•AWKWARD 2 the MAX!
•Who am I?

I'VE BEEN WRITING THE CHRONICLES OF MY LIFE. THAT'S MY UPDATED CAST PAGE.
HEY, I'M PRETTY COOL!
WE DIDN'T ABANDON YOU, DANY!
Did you cheat off me??
WHY AM I STRANGLING JOAN?
YOU'RE **HUGGING** HER!!
AT LEAST I GOT AN A+! ...YOU SPELLED CONCERTO WRONG.
OKAY, WOW, A LOT OF NOTES.
YOU'RE RIGHT, DANY. I **AM** TOO COOL FOR SCHOOL.
AND YET...
CHOCO
FLUTTER
← piece of tarp
MELTON MIDDLE SCHOOL
HERE WE ARE.
CAUTION Construction

WEREN'T THE REPAIRS SUPPOSED TO BE **DONE** BY NOW?
DO NOT ENTER
CAUTION
IT MIGHT TAKE THEM **YEARS** TO FIND FUNDING. THIS WAS PROBABLY **MILLIONS** OF DOLLARS OF DAMAGE.
EVERYONE IN CHEERLEADING HAS TO SELL FOUR BOXES OF GYM-REPAIR FUND-RAISING CHOCOLATES OR WE'RE OFF THE SQUAD.
CHOCOLATE, ANYONE?
rattle rattle
CHOCO
...AND WE'VE GOTTA ORGANIZE THE **SAVE MELTON DANCEATHON.**
A SCHOOL DANCE?!
THEY'RE ANNOUNCING IT TODAY. IT'S IN A WEEK OR SO.
CRUNCH
YOU'RE ALL COMING, I DON'T CARE WHO'S TOO COOL FOR DANCES, SO JUST ACCEPT IT.
GYM
WE'VE JUST GOTTA FIND A LOCATION, BECAUSE THE GYM IS A HAZARD ZONE.
CAUTION CAUTION
COUGH, COUGH. IF ONLY **SOME**ONE WOULD TAKE RESPONSIBILITY FOR THE GYM.
ME? HUH?
I...

meeting today! 3:15
TIP
TIP TIP TIP
I TOOK CARE OF THAT ALREADY!
TALKIN' BOUT MY EDUCATION!
ANY DAY NOW, THEY'RE GONNA PROCESS THAT MONEY AND RELEASE SOME **GLOWING STATEMENT** ABOUT THEIR RICH ANONYMOUS DONOR.
sigh...
AAAANY DAY NOW...
MY GYM TEACHER HAS JUST BEEN SHOWING US VIDEOS ABOUT... PUBERTY-RELATED SUBJECTS.
WHICH MY PARENTS WON'T LET ME WATCH, ANYWAY. THEY WROTE A **NOTE**.
CHOCO
IT'S **SO EMBARRASSING!** I JUST WANNA PLAY SOME BADMINTON--AND NOT IN THE PARKING LOT, EITHER!
...
Les Sad
•themes
•loaf
BE YOURSELF

English
Les Sad
·French
·Sad
·No singing
WHAT THEME IS JON VAL JON EXPRESSING ON PAGE 142?
DANIELLE?
I THINK JABERT IS IN LOVE WITH JON VAL JON!
WHY ELSE WOULD HE FOLLOW HIM TO THE ENDS OF THE EARTH?
BUT HIS RIGID IDEOLOGY WON'T ALLOW HIM... TO ACCEPT HIMSELF!
AMOUR
BAGUETTE
I DREW SOME FAN ART OF THEM OPENING A FRENCH BAKERY TOGETHER...
what?
PAIN
?
NO
BOOO
??
BOOOO
...lotta spare time...
C'MON, READING IS FUN! IT'S LIKE WATCHING A MOVIE IN YOUR... MIND? UM... THAT IS...
SIT DOWN!
BOO READING SUCKS
THAT IS, UH, I'M SORRY, I MISSPOKE; READING IS LAME...
SORRY FOR THE INTERRUPTION...
Grammar is SERIOUS
mutter mutter...

DANIELLE, I'M DISAPPOINTED IN YOU!
I THOUGHT YOU WERE A LITERARY-MINDED YOUNG LADY.
I THINK READING IS FUN, MRS. LECTOR!
YOU'RE WONDERFUL, MADISON.
...CARA TOLD ME SHE LIKES TO READ.
SIGH
hm...
DON'T DRAG ME INTO... WHATEVER THIS IS.
yeah
CAN WE GET BACK TO LEARNING?
GOOD IDEA, CARA.
CHEER
WOO!
clap clap
YEAH!!
CLAP CLAP
SHRINK

no one likes me
!!
You set my soul on fire.
You look like a glowing angel today.
I like you.
-secret admirer
BRINGGG

AHHH!!
FOOMP
Yikes!
CARA! CARA! DID YOU SEE ME?
hop

HOW 'BOUT WHEN I SPIKED IT, CARA?
SIGH...
MADISON! IT'S YOURS!
?!
FWOSHH
MADISON!!
?
I GOT IT!!!
FWOOSH
HIYA!!
FWOOOO
nice!

POM
HIGH 5!
AW, YEAH! TEAMWORK!
UH, CONGRATS? DO YOU WANT A MEDAL?
no...
HARUKA KANATA
I TOTALLY LOBBED THAT BALL-- YOU SAW?
...

I DIDN'T KNOW YOU'RE SUCH AN ATHLETE, DANY.
YOU'RE REALLY FLYING OUT THERE.
I DIDN'T REALIZE WE WERE PLAYING BY SPECIAL RULES.
competitive
heh... no...
YOU'RE DEAD.
A-ALEESHA?
FWOOO
WOW!
FSHEW!
POINT!
POINT!
no!!!
pff
oops...
SIGH...
you... you Killed Mr. Volleyball ...

...MRS. ROUGEAU IS PREGNANT AND SHE'S LETTING WHOEVER DOES BEST ON THE TEST NAME THE BABY!
I WANNA WIN!
WHAT IF IT'S YOU? WHAT WOULD YOU NAME THE BABY?
CLEOPATRA! COMIN' ATCHA!
...ANY NEW SECRETS YOU'RE WITHHOLDING FROM US TODAY, DANY?
heh...
WAIT, REALLY? I WAS JUST KIDDING. THE WORLD ISN'T IN DANGER, IS IT?
WHO DO WE GET TO FIGHT THIS TIME?
NAH, IT'S NOT LIKE THAT...
I JUST FOUND THIS NOTE IN MY LOCKER...

IS THAT--?!
JOAN
31
we rule the school
I DON'T KNOW WHO IT'S FROM.
WHOSE HANDWRITING IS THIS?!
WHAT IF IT'S TOM?
WOULD THAT BE... A GOOD THING?
?
sigh...
EH, I DUNNO.
YOU THINK **TOM** WOULD WRITE...?
MAYBE HE HAS A SECRET OOEY-GOOEY SENTIMENTAL SIDE. I CAN'T THINK OF ANYONE ELSE.
THERE'S... REALLY NO ONE ELSE I CAN THINK OF.

"YOU LOOK LIKE A **GLOWING ANGEL** TODAY."
I'M LIKE A CHRISTMAS TREE TOPPER!
YOU **DO** LOOK VERY DEWY TODAY.
AW, SHUCKS! THANKS, LEAH!
hmm
SUSPICIOUSLY DEWY.
LOOK! YOU'RE **LITERALLY GLOWING!** WHAT THE HECK!
FWIP
WELL... I CAME UP WITH THIS HANDY MAGICAL LIFE HACK...
OALS: STUDY ARDER
BEEP
BEEP
6:45 AM
UGHHH....
BEEP!!

nghh....
BEEEP—!
6:48
FLOP!
guh...
BY THE RAYS OF THE SUN... TRANSFORM...

ZZZZZ
DETANGLE!
NICE COMPLEXION
yawn
hrmph...
TOSS

HAIRY OTTER
NORMAL
DINGG!
Reminder: History essay due
NOW YOU TELL ME?!
I told you yesterday too.
7:10 AM
HISTORY ESSAY...
...THAT SEEMS LIKE I WROTE IT, BUT DID AN UNCHARACTERISTICALLY GOOD JOB.
SOMETHING THAT WILL MAKE MRS. MARKS...
...THINK I'M SMART.
POOF!
OH, AND MY MATH HOMEWORK TOO.

UGH. I'M SO TIRED.
SOLAR HEALING POWER. MAKE ME FEEL LIKE I'M NOT DYING.
WOMAN, YOU'RE MY WOMAN, I LOVED YOU ALL MY LIFE...
GOD, DAD! LEARN ANOTHER SONG ALREADY!
LAUREN, THAT'S OUR WEDDING SONG... KEEP PLAYING, CHUCK.
EMPEROR
yummy
WHEN WE MET, WE DIDN'T KNOW, THE DOG DAYS WE HAD AHEAD—
ha ha

BUT ALL I ASK IS THAT WE GROW CLOSER TOGETHER INSTEAD...
SWEETHEART! I LOVE IT!
CT POST
REVENGE
...DON'T YOU HAVE TO LEAVE FOR WORK SOON, CHUCK?
MILK
I TOLD THEM I'M NOT GOING IN TILL ELEVEN. IT'S SUCH A BEAUTIFUL DAY...
I CAN'T WAIT TO FINALLY QUIT THAT PLACE.
WHOSE BOWL IS THIS?
MOM! DAD! I'M TRYING TO **EAT** HERE!
Solve the Puzzle!
CHKK!
ORMAL
DANY, IS THAT YOUR BUS?
AHHHHHH!!!!
HEY! **DUMMY!** YOU FORGOT YOUR HOMEWORK!

MR. ROMANO, HUH? I HAD HIM. EASY A.
LAUREN! ARE YOU KIDDING ME?
IF YOU THINK PRE-ALGEBRA IS HARD... JUST WAIT FOR ACTUAL ALGEBRA. AND THEN PRECALC. AND CALC.
NOOO...
FIRST OUTER, INNER LAST. FOIL. IT'S SO EASY. I MISS WHEN MATH WAS EASY.
OH, YOU DEFINITELY MISSED THE BUS.
NO I DIDN'T! BYEEE!
DASH
LET ME KNOW IF YOU NEED A RIDE TO SCHOOL.
YOU'RE NOT GONNA EAT ANYTHING, LINDA?
I'M NOT HUNGRY.

FWOOSH
HI, DANY!
TAP O' THE MARNIN' TO YA, TOM!
HUH?
UH... "TOP OF THE MORNING TO YOU."
OH, YEAH. YOU TOO.

SO, DID YOU ALSO MISS THE BUS?
NOPE. FLYING IS JUST **SO** MUCH BETTER.
YEAH...
HEY, HOW COME NO ONE EVER NOTICES US **FLYING**? I THOUGHT I'D BE THE NEW **BIGFOOT** BY NOW. MELTON'S OWN FLYING BOY.
I THINK THE FLYING RINGS HAVE A CLOAKY SHIELD THINGY. IT WAS SOMEWHERE IN THE BACK OF MY MIND WHEN I DREW THEM.
WE'RE NOT **INVISIBLE**, BUT NO ONE WOULD EVER, LIKE, NOTICE US FLYING AROUND.
...I MEAN, WE CAN'T HAVE PEOPLE COMING AFTER US FOR OUR MAGIC!
WE'D HAVE TO FIGHT THE **GOVERNMENT**! THAT WOULD BE GNARLY!
GNARLY IN THE **BAD** WAY, MAYBE!
IT WOULD BE BOTH GNARLIES.

WOW, THAT PIECE OF TARP IS **NOT** DOING ITS JOB.
WE... WE REALLY WRECKED THE GYM, HUH.
FWOFF
...MEMORIES. OH, I'VE BEEN PRACTICING SOLAR PUNCH! CHECK IT OUT!
BY THE RAYS OF THE SUN, TRANSFORM!
SOLAR PUNCH! SOLAR PUNCH!
oooh!

PLUCK
THAT IS SO COOL!
I'M REALLY STARTING TO GET A HANG OF THE CONTROLS.
ha ha
PINECONE?
THANKS!
I'VE COME UP WITH A FEW USES FOR SOLAR FLARE MYSELF.

LIKE CHARGING MY LAPTOP...
...DOING HOUSEHOLD TASKS...
VRRRRRR
...YA KNOW, BASICALLY INVENTING NEW KINDS OF LAZY.
FLICK
...THAT'S WHAT THEY CALL "THE ROOT OF HUMAN INNOVATION."
WOW...
CAN YOU MAKE FIREWORKS WITH YOUR POWERS? YOU SHOULD DEFINITELY MAKE FIREWORKS.
OOH! I WONDER!

TO DANY
SHIK!
DO YOU KNOW WHICH QUESTIONS WE--
AGHH! **NO!!** LEAVE ME ALONE, ***DEMON!***
PHEW! CLOSE ENCOUNTERS OF THE ***RUDE*** KIND.
A ***BOY*** WROTE ***YOU*** A ***LOVE NOTE?***

REALLY.
YEAH.
yeah
WAIT, BUT READ THIS ONE UP CLOSE--
"YOU'RE SWEAT AND GORGEOUS"?
yeah
WELL, HE GOT ONE PART RIGHT.
I THINK HE MEANT "SWEET."
SWEAT AND GORGEOUS!
hoo o ha ha
BUT LIKE, AM I EVEN "SWEET"?
NORMAL
SIGH...
HE ALSO SAID, "YOU'RE THE ONLY ONE WHO SEES ME." SO I MAY BE COMMUNING WITH A GHOST.
ha ha
ha ha
SWEAT AND GORGEOUS!
I DON'T THINK I'D LIKE A BOY WHO CAN'T EVEN SPELL "SWEET."
EDWARD YANG ALMOST BEAT ME AT THE SPELLING BEE.
ULTIMATELY I DESTROYED HIM, OF COURSE.
WANT ME TO ASK HIM IF HE LIKES YOU?
ha ha
YOU BETTER NOT!!!

OH, MADISON, I'M THINKING OF HAVING ALL THE GIRLS COME OVER THIS WEEKEND. WE CAN PRACTICE OUR ROUTINES...
I WAS TALKING TO COACH AND SHE SAID IF WE DON'T GET ENOUGH PRACTICE, WE WON'T MAKE IT ANYWHERE **NEAR** THE CHAMPIONSHIP. ARE YOU FREE?
yeah
GOOD IDEA! NOT GONNA LIE, I FORGOT HOW TO DO THE SCORPION.
DON'T DO THE SCORPION! YOU COULD GET STUNG!
HARDY HAR HAR.
WOW, DANY, YOU HAVE A HILARIOUS REPLY TO **EVERYTHING.**
TH... THAT'S ME!
WHAT IS **THAT** SUPPOSED TO MEAN?
SHE'S JUST ALWAYS **HERE.** CHUCKLING IT UP. IT'S **ANNOYING.** NO OFFENSE.
yeah

THAT'S SO RUDE.
BUT I **SAID** "NO OFFENSE"!
OH MY GOD, DANY CAN TAKE IT. RIGHT, DANY?
IT'S COOL, I'M COOL. I CAN GET ALONG WITH MY FELLOW CLASSMATES.
NORMAL
ANYWAY, MADISON, ARE YOU AROUND THIS WEEKEND?
YOU'RE A JERK. C'MON, DANY.
MADISON, WHY ARE YOU STARTING A FIGHT OUT OF NOTHING?
IT'S NOT **NOTHING!** SHE CAN'T TALK TO MY **BEST FRIEND** LIKE THAT! I'LL QUIT CHEERLEADING JUST TO **SPITE** HER.
I-IN HER DEFENSE, WHAT IS CARA SUPPOSED TO DO IF I ANNOY HER? JUST SILENTLY PUT UP WITH IT FOREVER?
WAIT, WHY ARE YOU ON **HER** SIDE?
IF SOME ANNOYING DORKY GIRL STARTED SITTING WITH ME AND INTERJECTING DUMB JOKEY COMMENTARY, I MIGHT WANT HER TO LEAVE ME ALONE TOO.

IT'S KINDA HARD TO BE ON YOUR SIDE WHEN **YOU'RE** NOT EVEN ON YOUR SIDE.
I'M SORRY...
MAYBE I'M OVERREACTING. MAYBE IT'S JUST MY ***FRIENDSHIP PROGRAMMING*** KICKING IN.
MADISON. YOU CAN'T JUST RAGE-QUIT ***CHEERLEADING***! THAT WOULDN'T HELP ***ANYONE.***
I CAN DO WHATEVER I ***CHOOSE.***
CRAP! I LEFT MY BACKPACK IN THE CAFETERIA!
BRRING
NORMAL
SEE YOU IN CLASS.
TRASH
VEND
WHO WOULD JUST... THROW AWAY MY BACKPACK...
TRASH
TO THINE OWN ELF BE TRUE
HONESTLY...

SNIFF...
I DON'T KNOW HOW YOU'VE CONNED MADISON INTO BEING YOUR FRIEND.
AND ALEESHA TOO. THEY'RE MY FRIENDS. YOU CAN'T JUST... INSERT YOURSELF.
I'M SORRY I'M ANNOYING. MY FRIENDS TOLD ME TO "BE MYSELF," AND I INEXPLICABLY LISTENED TO THEIR ADVICE.
YOU KNOW WHAT, IT'S ACTUALLY SWEET OF YOU TO APOLOGIZE.
BUT IT DOESN'T CHANGE THE FACT THAT YOU'RE-- LIKE, YOU'RE WEARING A SHIRT THAT SAYS "NORMAL"?
IS THE JOKE THAT YOU'RE WEIRD?!
...I JUST THOUGHT IT WAS FUNNY.
NORMAL
MADISON SAID SHE'D QUIT CHEERLEADING IF YOU DIDN'T APOLOGIZE TO ME. YOU DON'T HAVE TO--
ME? APOLOGIZE TO YOU? SO I CAN'T EVEN SAY WHAT I THINK ANYMORE?
I GUESS YOU WERE... UNAWARE OF MY EXTREMELY SENSITIVE FEELINGS--
SHE'D QUIT CHEERLEADING OVER SOMETHING THIS STUPID?!
LOOK, I DON'T WANT HER TO DO IT EITHER--

NO? WELL, IT SURE **SEEMS** LIKE MADISON DOES WHATEVER YOU SAY.
N-NO SHE DOESN'T!
WE CUT SARAHLEE FROM THE TEAM FOR MADISON. SARAHLEE EVEN HAD HER WIDDLE **MOMMY** CALL UP THE SCHOOL TO COMPLAIN ABOUT IT! (WHAT A LOSER!)
I COULD **RUIN** MADISON AT THIS SCHOOL, IF I WANTED TO.
I CAN RUIN YOU TOO, ALTHOUGH IT'S NOT LIKE YOU'VE GOT MUCH OF A REPUTATION TO KEEP OTHER THAN "LOCKER WHISPERER."
GEEZ, CARA!!! I'D **PAY** YOU NOT TO DO THAT.
RECOIL!
THAT WORKS FOR ME.
WAIT, REALLY?
DO YOU ACTUALLY **HAVE** ANY MONEY?
I DO! UHH, MY PARENTS WON THE LOTTO.
I'LL BUY **ALL** YOUR CHOCOLATES. THEN YOU'LL LIKE ME?

JUST PRETEND TO BE MY FRIEND WHEN MADISON'S AROUND!
NORMAL
SO, THIS IS HOW YOU MAKE FRIENDS?
heh
IS THAT WHY MADISON'S FRIENDS WITH YOU? IT'S FINALLY STARTING TO MAKE SENSE.
SLUMP
MADISON AND I ARE FRIENDS BECAUSE... WE JUST ARE.
NORMAL
CHOCO
SHE'S NOT, LIKE... INDEBTED TO ME OR ANYTHING.
COOL! I HAD NO IDEA YOU WERE RICH.
CHOCO
TODAY IS AWESOME!
NORMAL

CAUTION
CAUTION
DO
NOT
Danielle,
you're the only
who sees me.
are sweat
gorgeous
Secret
Admirer
TO
DANY
BRRINGGG
...SO I'M WASHING OFF MY BACKPACK, AND CARA COMES IN.
UGH. **CARA.**

YOU CAN'T BE MAD AT HER ANYMORE! SHE APOLOGIZED TO ME-- SHE WAS SO NICE ABOUT IT--
REALLY?
YEAH! WELL, I JUST TOLD HER, LIKE, "YOU HURT MY FEELINGS. AND THAT'S NOT OKAY."
I'M PROUD OF YOU! YEAH, SHE NEEDS TO LEARN TO RESPECT YOU.
SHE WON'T DO IT IF YOU'RE APOLOGIZING TO HER WHEN SHE'S MEAN TO YOU.
...
ALL YOU NEED IS MORE TIME TOGETHER. JUST TO GET TO KNOW EACH OTHER.
I DUNNO ABOUT THAT.
CHOLO
...YOU CAN HELP US ORGANIZE THE SAVE MELTON DANCEATHON.
...
I DON'T... UH...
I'LL CONVINCE THE BOTH OF YOU.

You can't talk to me like that!!
You're right! I'm SO sorry!
no no no
I can talk to you how I want! You wanna see mean? You haven't seen MEAN YET!!
MADISON!
You don't deserve to be Madison's friend!
LIAR!
You paid off Cara to be friends with you??
It backfired and I'm stealing your magic!
WHY am I thinking like this??
Anyone home?
silence...
WHAT A TERRIBLE MEMOIR.
THUNK!
I HATE THE MAIN CHARACTER.
FLOP

HOW CAN I EVER GO BACK TO SCHOOL? AND PRETEND EVERYTHING IS FINE?
AND SIT WITH **CARA** AT LUNCH WHEN SHE **OOZES ANNOYANCE** AT MY **VERY EXISTENCE?**
AND IF I SIT WITH **TOM,** MADISON WILL KNOW CARA AND I DIDN'T REALLY MAKE UP.
AND I'LL BE LIKE, "I LIED? CARA HATES ME?"
AND THEN **MADISON** WILL HATE ME TOO.
ORMA
AND WHAT IF SITTING WITH TOM IS ACTUALLY SECRETLY **ANNOYING** BUT HE'S TOO NICE TO SAY SO?
WHAT IF I'M ANNOYING **MADISON** AND **SHE'S** TOO NICE TO SAY SO?
WHAT IF THAT'S MY WHOLE LIFE FOREVER UNTIL I DIE?!

IF ONLY I HAD A CLONE.
IF I HAD A CLONE, SHE COULD SOLVE **ALL** MY PROBLEMS.
I will help!
BUT IF SHE'S ME, WOULDN'T SHE HAVE ALL THE SAME PROBLEMS?
NO! NOT IF I COULD... **IMPROVE** ON THE ORIGINAL.
FLIP
STILL **ME,** OTHERWISE WHAT'S THE POINT?
BUT LIKE... PERHAPS SOME CONFIDENCE. THAT'D BE NICE. WHAT A CONCEPT.
OOH!
SHE COULD BE...
SECRETLY...
A **PIKKIMAL!** SO I KEEP HER IN A PIKKIBALL WHEN SHE'S NOT IN USE. THAT WAY NO ONE FINDS OUT!
HAH! NAILED IT!
POOF

"PIKKIBALL, GO!"
WHERE AM I?
AHH!! PIKKIBALL, GO!
OW! HEY!
CLÖN LABS
LAB
DANY?
HELLO, ME.
GAH! SORRY! I FREAKED OUT.
LET ME EXPLAIN.
I THINK I GET IT! I'M LIKE, YOUR LIFE DISASTER CONSULTANT. CLONE EDITION.
SO THIS IS WHAT I LOOK LIKE TO EVERYONE? AND SOUND LIKE? MY VOICE SOUNDS SO WEIRD.
I KNOW, RIGHT?

YOU LIKE WHAT YOU SEE? ♥
SPIN AROUND!
SPIN♥
WOW! IT'S LIKE-- I'M JUST ANOTHER PERSON! I GUESS I ALWAYS KNEW THAT, BUT...
I WANNA SEE!
WOW, THERE IT IS! THE BACK OF MY HEAD! JUST LIKE I'D ALWAYS IMAGINED.
hee hee
TADA!!
SPIN!
WILL YOU DO MY HOMEWORK?
YEAH, TOTALLY. I'LL DO IT LATER!
WHAT'S IT LIKE INSIDE THE PIKKIBALL, CLONEY?
WOULD YOU LIKE THE GRAND TOUR?
NORMAL
YEAH!
CLICK!
BRZZT

whoa...
WELCOME
ICE
WELCOME
OPEN 24hr
ART SUPPLIES
HOW DO YOU LIKE IT?
FWUMP
EVERYTHING HERE IS MADE OUT OF BEDS! IT'S AWESOME!
CLOCKMEN
INFINITE JOKES
DFW
By the Shores of Silver Lake
TOILETS OF THE SEA
AND LOOK AT ALL THESE BOOKS! THEY'RE ALL THE BOOKS I'VE BEEN MEANING TO CHECK OUT!

OOH!!
Chatty Lady's Gentleman Caller
THESE ARE ALL THE BOOKS MOM SAID I CAN'T READ...
BIRDS
ARE YOU THERE, GOD? IT'S ME, MARIO!
Modern fantasy
BANNED
GIRD YOUR LOINS! Lurid descriptions of the female ankle shocked Victorian audiences when book was banned
WOW!
AWESOME, RIGHT? MAKE YOURSELF AT HOME.
The Public Garden
STARSHIPS
LORD OF THE RUNGS
Babysitting Cubs
GO YELL IT FROM A MOUNTAIN
ANGELA'S RASHES
Wild Magic T. Pierce
DRUCY NAN
WUH-WHAT IS THIS?!
YOU KNOW WHAT IT IS.
FLOPP
NO ONE CAN KNOW OF MY CRUSH!!!! I WILL GO TO THE GRAVE WITH THIS SECRET!!! IT'S TOO EMBARRASSING!!!
I KNOW. I'LL JUST DIE IF ANYONE FINDS OUT.

HE'S SO CUTE. LOOK AT THIS ONE--
memory.exe
no forks!
Puppies
IT'S HIS HAIR. HE HAS COOL HAIR.
yeah...
HE LOVES SCI-FI AND POETRY...
Poems About Aliens
HE'S ALSO NICE...
you can copy my homework
yay!
HW
I BET HE'S REALLY DEEP. I CAN JUST TELL.
DEEP
• thoughts
• eyes
• soul
TOTALLY! HE SAID SOMETHING THIS MORNING-- UH--

memory.exe
Pinecone
SO DEEP!
"[LAZINESS IS] THE ROOT OF HUMAN INNOVATION."
HE'S NOT THE CLASSICAL, GET-GOOD-GRADES TYPE... MORE OF A...
CLÖN LABS
MISUNDERSTOOD GENIUS. JUST LIKE US. HEHEHE.
HE WOULDN'T SPELL "SWEET" WRONG, WOULD HE?
M-MAYBE HIS HAND SLIPPED WHEN HE WAS WRITING.
YEAH.
ELCOME
ICE
WOW... YOU HAVE A FOOD FOUNTAIN...
I ALSO HAVE CRIME STREETS 3.
LET'S SEE WHO'S A BETTER STREET CRIMINAL!
CLONE VS. Dany classic

3 HOURS LATER
WOW, YOU'RE REALLY GOOD AT CRIME STREETS!
BUT, CLONEY, YOU TOTALLY CREAMED ME!
I GUESS I'M... REALLY REALLY GOOD.
CLONES RULE!
I got BLISTERS on me fingers!!
OW!!
ha ha we're hilarious
YOU KNOW, I DON'T KNOW WHAT'S WRONG WITH CARA. I'M SO MUCH FUN TO HANG OUT WITH!
braiding our hair together
YAY
ha ha
FUN
LOL
ME TOO! I AGREE! HAHAHA!
YOU WOULD AGREE, WOULDN'T YOU, CLONEY!

OH YEAH. WE'RE DEFINITELY ON THE SAME PAGE. HOW ABOUT YOU CHILL OUT HERE AND I'LL DO YOUR HOMEWORK AS A LITTLE THANK-YOU FOR BRINGING ME INTO THIS WORLD.
sounds like a plan!
THIS WAS A QUESTIONABLE DECISION.
wah
VR WORKOUT
HAMSTER WHEEL EDITION
IMAGINE YOU'RE NOT EXERCISING!
LVL 1: CENTAURED + BALANCED
WELCOME
SINK
OCT.
COULD YOU HELP ME WITH SOME--
OH, DANY, YOU'RE ACTUALLY DOING YOUR HOMEWORK! I'M SO PROUD OF YOU!

UM, MOM? DO YOU KNOW HOW TO FOIL?
Uh–
$(3x-4)(2x+1)$
YOU JUST... SEE, X IS...
WHY DON'T YOU EVER ASK ME FOR HELP WITH THE FUN STUFF, LIKE YOUR ENGLISH HOMEWORK?
THAT'S CUZ IT'S EASY!
ASK YOUR SISTER!
I'M GOING OUT WITH MY FRIENDS. MY MATH NOTES FROM SEVENTH GRADE ARE IN THE BASEMENT, THOUGH.
Nah.
UGH, I GIVE UP!
DANY'S ROOM STAY OUT
POOF
BOOOOO!
C'MON, DANY, YOU CAN DO IT!
WELL, I TRIED.

I CAN'T HAVE THREE OF US RUNNING AROUND!
MAYBE YOU SHOULD MAKE ANOTHER CLONE. LIKE, A REALLY SCHOLARLY ONE.
...SHE'D PROBABLY BE LAZY, TOO!
YOU READY FOR YOUR FIRST DAY OF SCHOOL?
I GUESS SO! TIME TO TAKE THE WORLD BY STORM!
hug
MY DAUGHTER... THEY GROW UP SO FAST.
you got this
OKAY, I'LL BE IN THE PIKKIBALL IF YOU NEED ME.

Danny R. Science
POP QUIZ
YAWN
grumble
CLÖN LABS
EGGS
You selected
sunny side up
scrambled
scrambled eggs
HARD BOILED
FRENCH TOAST
PUSH
what's the answer to this?
DANIELLE?
HISTORY
ROBBER BARONS!!
That's not what I was looking for, but actually a fascinating response—
snort
HISTORY
I COULD STAY IN HERE AND NEVER LEAVE.
CLÖN LABS
YOU SURE ABOUT THAT? I MIGHT GO ROGUE AND TAKE OVER YOUR LIFE FOREVER.
HAH! GO FOR IT.

HA
AUDITORIUM
VEND
DANY, I'M THIRSTY. BE A **PAL** AND GO GET ME A **DIET LEMON CHELTZER.**
?
WHY ME?
LOOK, IF YOU REALLY WANNA BE **COOL...**
It's a test!
...YOU'LL GET ME A CHELTZER.
GET THE CHELTZER!
WHAT IF I GET YOU ONE IN THE CAF? MADISON AND ALEESHA ARE ABANDONING US.
UGH. **FINE.**

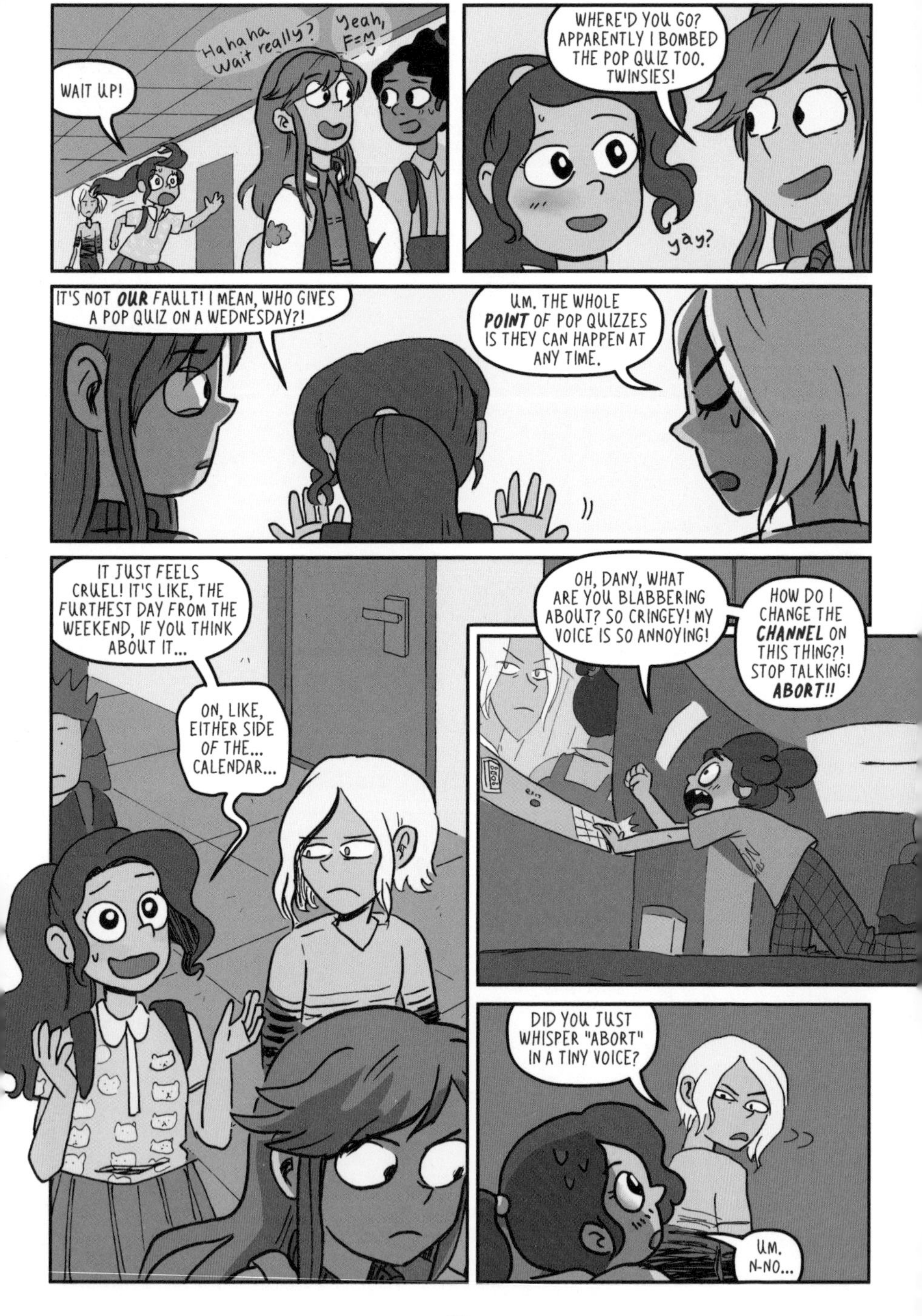

WAIT UP!
Hahaha wait really?
Yeah, F=M
WHERE'D YOU GO? APPARENTLY I BOMBED THE POP QUIZ TOO. TWINSIES!
yay?
IT'S NOT **OUR** FAULT! I MEAN, WHO GIVES A POP QUIZ ON A WEDNESDAY?!
UM. THE WHOLE **POINT** OF POP QUIZZES IS THEY CAN HAPPEN AT ANY TIME.
IT JUST FEELS CRUEL! IT'S LIKE, THE FURTHEST DAY FROM THE WEEKEND, IF YOU THINK ABOUT IT...
ON, LIKE, EITHER SIDE OF THE... CALENDAR...
OH, DANY, WHAT ARE YOU BLABBERING ABOUT? SO CRINGEY! MY VOICE IS SO ANNOYING!
HOW DO I CHANGE THE **CHANNEL** ON THIS THING?! STOP TALKING! **ABORT!!**
DID YOU JUST WHISPER "ABORT" IN A TINY VOICE?
UM. N-NO...

self mute
ACK! HOW CAN I RUIN THINGS FROM INSIDE THE PIKKIBALL?! I'M SORRY, CLONEY!
MENU
Sighhh...
SPORT 1 TEAM
...SO BY THAT POINT, HE'S COMPLETELY UNDERWATER, BUT HE JUST KEEPS--
guh...

...ANYWAY, IT WAS PRETTY HILARIOUS AT THE TIME.
ha ha me
DID SOMEONE ORDER A CHELTZER?
...I THOUGHT THE QUIZ WAS **EASY**.
PTHHT!
SO EASY, I DID IT IN MY SLEEP!
I **SAW** THAT!
...I SLEPT THROUGH THE QUIZ!
DANY! THAT'S TERRIBLE!
ha ha
IS THAT SOMETHING YOU'RE **PROUD** OF?
WHAT A FOOL I WAS!
I'm... annoying.

OH MY GOD, SHUUUT UP!
...WHAT? I HAVE SENSITIVE EARS.
guh...
TOSS!
YA BLEW IT!
I THOUGHT YOU GUYS MADE UP.
WE DID, WE DID.
WHERE ARE YOU GOING? COME BACK.
BACK AWAY
I DON'T WANT TO FEEL LIKE I'M TALKING ON EGGSHELLS, SO--
WHAT ARE YOU **TALKING** ABOUT?
yeah
Dany?
CHOCO
IT'S A PLAY ON WORDS! PEACE OUT!
fury & loathing
mild sympathy
NONONO! TURN BACK AND **GROVEL!**
YOU CAN'T TALK TO CARA LIKE THAT! SHE'LL DESTROY US!

MAYBE CARA HATES PUNS.
TALKING ON EGGSHELLS... MAN, I THOUGHT THAT WAS A WINNER.
OR US.
HEY, TOM AND ELDER MATT! WHAT'S...?
nice Pikkiball
I FORGOT TO DO MY MATH HOMEWORK, SO I'M JUST WRITING DOWN RANDOM NUMBERS...
SCOOT
DO YOU THINK HE CHECKS THE ANSWERS?
CORN JUICE*
YOU CAN COPY MINE.

I DIDN'T DO IT EITHER...
IF YA KNOW WHAT I MEAN.
WINK★
ALERT!!
WINK ACTIVATED
OH MY GOD, YOU DID NOT JUST **WINK!!!**
OH, GOOD, THAT MEANS THE ANSWERS WILL ACTUALLY BE RIGHT THIS TIME!
ha ha
...TROUBLE AT THE GIRL TABLE AGAIN?
YEAH. CARA MCCOY TOTALLY HATES ME.
shrug
WHAT HAPPENED?
SHE SEEMS TO HAVE AN ISSUE WITH MY...
LOUD VOICE...
AMONG OTHER THINGS...

YOU'RE NOT SO BAD. THE CAFETERIA IS LOUD. VOLUME IS RELATIVE.
YOU'RE JUST BOISTEROUS.
...THINK IT HAS SOMETHING TO DO WITH MADISON?
MATH
I DUNNO. MAYBE.
IF ONLY CARA KNEW THE... SPECIAL CIRCUMSTANCES... OF MY FRIENDSHIP WITH MADISON...
THAT SHOULD PROBABLY BE MADISON'S CALL, THOUGH, RIGHT?
WASH YOUR LUNCH
YEAH.
HERE'S THE THING: I LITERALLY PAID CARA TO PRETEND TO BE MY FRIEND, SO I FEEL OWED JUST A SLIVER OF RESPECT FROM HER.
ha
ha
lame...
IF NOT REAL RESPECT, THEN PRETEND RESPECT AT LEAST.
heh heh

YOU SHOULD SEE IF YOU CAN GET A REFUND. THAT'S **BREACH OF CONTRACT.**
DANY! YOU'RE AIRING OUR DIRTY LAUNDRY...
DID YOU HEAR PRINCIPAL FLINSKY IS RETIRING? HE GOT SOME HUGE INHERITANCE.
WHAT?!!
SLAM
HE'S MOVING TO A RANCH IN ARIZONA.
you ARE loud...
THAT'S NOT RIGHT! **RETIREMENT?!** THE MAN IS, WHAT, FORTY-FIVE?!
HE SHOULD USE HIS "INHERITANCE" TO PAY FOR THE **GYM REPAIRS.**
WHY WOULD HE--
OHHH.
WAIT, WHY WOULD HE PAY FOR GYM REPAIRS OUT OF HIS OWN PERSONAL FUNDS?
WHAT AM I MISSING HERE? ARE YOU HINTING AT SOMETH-
NOTHING.

IT'S JUST FOR THE GREATER GOOD?! HE DIDN'T EARN THAT MONEY. IT JUST FELL IN HIS LAP.
YEAH. IT'S LIKE SPIDERBAT SAYS: "WITH GREAT WEALTH COMES A LOT OF RESPONSIBILITY."
YOU GUYS ARE CRAZY.
Yeah!
SPIDERBAT'S LIFE LESSONS ASIDE, PRINCIPAL FLINSKY CAN DO WHATEVER HE WANTS WITH HIS MONEY AS LONG AS WE LIVE IN A CAPITALIST SOCIETY.
BRRINGGG
boo capitalism!
bye
see ya, bud
I FEEL LIKE WE HAVE RESPONSIBILITIES TOO.
r-responsibility??
LIKE, WHY ELSE WOULD WE HAVE THESE AMAZING POWERS?

OH! YEAH. THAT COULD BE FUN. WE SHOULD...
...WE SHOULD, LIKE, PRACTICE OUR SOLAR POWERS™ AND SCOUT FOR VILLAINY TOGETHER SOMETIME.
YOU **WHAT?!** AHH!!!!
ACK!
THAT'D BE RAD!!!
WHAT?
PLUS ULTRA!
ha ha
hey watch it
SINK

WELCOME
PHEW. HOMEWORK TIME. I CAN DO THIS.
REALLY I'LOVE MY FAMILY
7th Grade
LAUREN'S MATH NOTES! NICE!
SUDS of ANARCHY LAUNDRY DETERGENT
ROMANO. MATH. 7th Gr. L. RADLEY
MATH
GYM

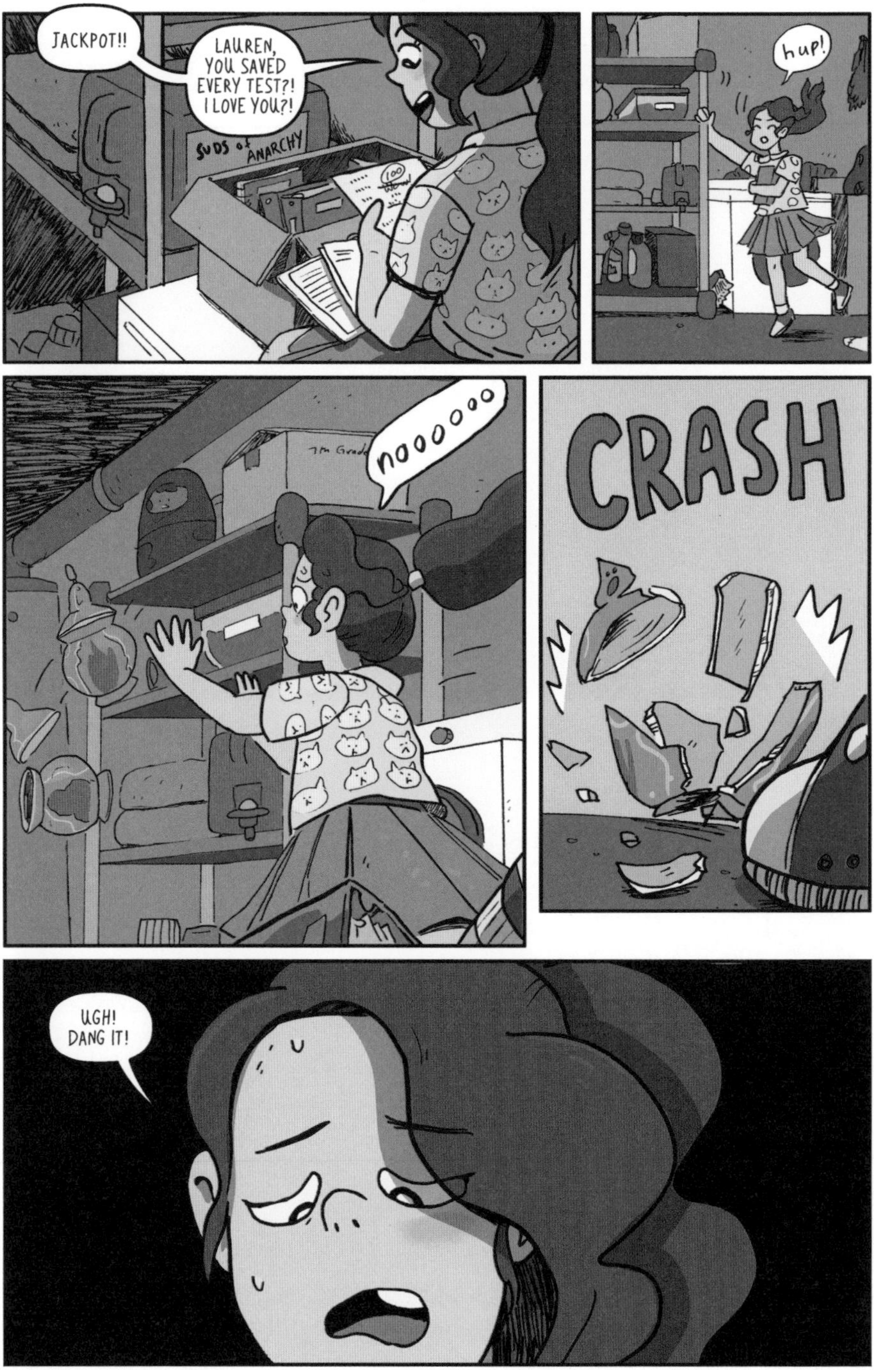
JACKPOT!!
LAUREN, YOU SAVED EVERY TEST?! I LOVE YOU?!
SUDS of ANARCHY
hup!
7th Grade
nooooooo
CRASH
UGH! DANG IT!

WAH?
WOO WOO WOO
WOOF!
WOOF! WOOF!
Puppy?♥
SKIDD!

7th grade
hrf
hrf
WE HAVE A DOG?
BRZZT

THE DOOR!
SALAMI?
Sniff
UH... WHAT DID I JUST DO?!
I DUNNO, CLONEY.
CLÖN LABS

PUPPYYY COME BACKKK...
I CAN'T TELL WHICH DIRECTION IT WENT!
I— DIDN'T MEAN TO MESS UP...
NO... IT'S OKAY...
I'M THE WORST CLONE EVER!
HEY, HEY, WE CAN HANDLE THIS! DON'T CRY, CLONEY!
WE'LL FIGURE THIS OUT.
FWOOOO
FSHHHH

PTHT!
STIR
SHADY MEN? I GUESS IT IS AN EMERGENCY.
THEY'LL FIX THE SALAMI DOOR.
WE SHOULD SEND ONE TO LOOK FOR THE BLUE DOG!
YEAH!
SEEK YE THE DOG WITH PELT OF BLUE.
WHO'D HAVE THOUGHT WE'D EVEN NEED AN ARMY OF TEMPORARY MUD-BASED AUTOMATONS?

(The day Prince Neptune tried to conquer Connecticut)
OH NO, THE FIRE DEPARTMENT IS HERE...
WEEOOWEEOOWEEOO
EVERYONE SAW ME! THEY ALL KNOW MY SECRET... WHAT DO I DO?
THE TRUTH WILL SET YOU FREE.
NOT IN THIS SCENARIO! NOT IF THEY TELL THE **GROWN-UPS** THAT I HAVE **MAGIC!**
DETRANSFORM, LEAH! DON'T LET THEM SEE YOU LIKE THAT!
WHY DON'T WE JUST TURN BACK TIME OR SOMETHING?
GEE, MADISON, THAT'S A BIT DRASTIC?
I'VE GOT IT! WE CAN...
WE CAN JUST WIPE EVERYONE'S MINDS.
JUST OF THE GYM BATTLE. SOFTEN THEIR MEMORIES WITH SOME ENCHANTED FREE T-SHIRTS.
NO ONE CAN RESIST FREE T-SHIRTS!
skrtch
POOF
?
...AND WE CAN HAVE THESE **MUD CREATURES** HAND OUT THE SHIRTS!!
MUD...?
Bag o' Shirts

ARE YOU KIDDING ME?! NO WAY! YOU CAN'T MESS WITH PEOPLE'S BRAINS LIKE THAT!
YOU WOULD BRAINWASH THE PUBLIC?! WHAT ARE YOU, A SUPERVILLAIN?!
I GUESS IT'S LIKE, WHAT THEY DON'T KNOW WON'T HURT THEM...
FWIP
FWIP
AAHH!
FWIP
hey!
Free T-shirt...
METEOR
ha
ha ha ha ha
MELTON METEOR

WHAT DO YOU THINK THAT BLUE DOG WAS? WHY WAS IT IN A BOTTLE?
WHAT WOULD OUR PARENTS WANT WITH BOTTLED DOG?
mmm
DO YOU THINK THEY KNOW ABOUT... MAGIC?
I DESPERATELY DON'T WANT THEM TO, BUT... SIGNS POINT TO... SOMETHING.
MAYBE WE SHOULD SPLIT UP AND LOOK FOR THIS DOG?
Good idea...
SIGH...

...OOH, WHAT IF YOUR **DAD** CHAPERONES THE SCHOOL DANCE. WHEN'S HE BACK FROM NEW YORK?
I DON'T KNOW.
YOGA FOR GOOD GRADES
HE'S GOT AN APARTMENT IN MIDTOWN. HIS OFFICE NEEDS HIM ALL THE TIME.
NOT THAT **MOM** EVEN CARES.
MAYBE YOU CAN VISIT HIM. HAVE A *FUN* DAY IN THE CITY TOGETHER.
...WOULD YOU COME WITH ME?
SURE.

I THINK MADISON'S IN THE LIVING ROOM.
THANKS, SKYE!
MADISON! LEVEL 100 EMERGENCY!
BURST
FLAIL
WHA-?!
THUNK

Breathe into your Spine...
OH, UH, NEVER MIND.
HHHI, CARA.
WHAT HAPPENED?!
OH, UH, LEVEL 100 IS THE LOWEST LEVEL. LEVEL 1 IS THE HIGHEST LEVEL. IT'S, UH, THE METRIC SYSTEM.
TELL ME.
CARA? I'VE GOTTA HELP DANY WITH A THING.
FINE, I'LL SEE YOU LATER.

CARA? HUH? WHERE'S MADISON?
SHE JUST **LEFT** WITH YOU! WHAT DO **I** KNOW?!
AAAAHHH BYE
DASH
UGH! WHY IS **THAT** GIRL HERE?!
SAD DEATH
FOR REAL.
I CAN'T BELIEVE YOU FREAKIN' **CLONED** YOURSELF.
ACTUALLY, NO, I **CAN**. I JUST WISH YOU'D ASKED ME FOR ADVICE INSTEAD.
YOU WOULD'VE STOPPED ME!
...EXACTLY!
I CAN'T BELIEVE MY PARENTS HAD A BOTTLED DOG!
WHAT'S UP WITH THAT?

WHAT IS THE FUNCTION OF A BLUE DOG IN A BOTTLE?
BEATS ME. DAD ALWAYS SAYS NO DOGS ALLOWED.
...WHICH IS JUST **SO** HYPOCRITICAL NOW.
WOL·MORT
BUT HE DOESN'T EVEN **LIKE** DOGS, SO IT DOESN'T REALLY ADD UP...
GAS
WHERE DO YOU THINK THEY GOT IT?
IT MUST HAVE COME FROM GREAT-AUNT ELMA'S ESTATE. I MEAN, THAT'S WHERE I GOT MY MAGIC **SKETCHBOOK**...
GIMME
...AND THIS DOG SOMEHOW TURNED THE BACK DOOR INTO **SALAMI!**
WANT SOME?
SKYE AND REX ARE PESCATARIANS.
I'M SO SORRY.
MMM, THIS IS GOOD SALAMI.
EVER PUT SALAMI IN THE MICROWAVE? IT'S REALLY GOOD.
OH?
OH MY GOD... UNRELATED, BUT DIDN'T YOUR PARENTS JUST WIN THE ***CASH4LYFE LOTTO***?

YEAH...
AND YOUR MOM, SHE LOST A TON OF WEIGHT--
SHE WENT ON, LIKE...
...A CRASH DIET... IT WAS REALLY SUDDEN...
DOG GENIE!!
THEY **WOULDN'T**...
NO?
OH MY GOD. DOG GENIE.

whistle
...YOUR MOTHER LETS YOU DYE YOUR HAIR PINK?
I'M AN ORPHAN!
MELTON ANIMAL CONTROL
THE ANIMAL SHELTER WAS PRETTY PSYCHED ABOUT THAT $2 MILLION DONATION FROM OUR "ECCENTRIC GREAT-AUNT."
HAH. NICE COVER STORY. I BET THEY THINK WE'RE IN THE MOB.
...GUH, I NEED A COVER STORY! WHAT LIE DO I TELL MY PARENTS IF--
DOG PARK
MAYBE WE CAN EXPLAIN IT TO THEM. YOUR PARENTS ARE PRETTY CHILL.
NOT REALLY. THEY'RE ALWAYS MAD AT ME AND TELLING ME WHAT TO DO.
nice!
ruff ruff
DOG PARK
REX AND SKYE WOULD NEVER TELL ME WHAT TO DO.
THAT'S COOL.
KISS
PET
NAH, IT'S JUST AWKWARD.

IT'S LIKE... WE ALL KNOW THEY'RE NOT MY PARENTS. NOT REALLY.
SO THEY CAN'T YELL AT ME. IT'S LIKE I'M A HOUSEGUEST.
BUT I CAN'T ACT OUT--
HEY!
CHOMP
That's him!!
CONTROL YOUR STUPID DOG!
SPRINT
STAY!!
FWOO

I wish I had REAL PARENTS!
BRUFF!
You are not my master.
BING BING BING
6:03
Mama Bear
yesterday
Do we have potatoes?
Yeah
Thanks
now
WHERE R U??
OMG
COME HOME NOW!!
...
FWOOF
sparkly...

DANIELLE!
WARP
WHAT DID YOU DO?!?!
Y-YOU DON'T NEED TO WITNESS THIS.
SQUEEZE
GET IN HERE!
WHY ARE YOU HERE, MADISON?
hey Linda
SO YOUR MAGIC DOG GENIE RAN AWAY. LOOKS LIKE YOUR WISHES STUCK AROUND, THOUGH.
MADISON!
YOU KNOW ABOUT MAGIC?! ABOUT THE HINN?!

OH, I KNOW ABOUT MAGIC.
ahem
I KNOCKED OVER THE LAMP AND THE DOG CAME OUT.
PUSH AWAY
M
WELL, WHERE DID IT GO?
IT RAN AWAY! MADISON AND I WERE TRYING TO CATCH IT!
I– I THOUGHT WE REALLY COVERED OUR TRACKS--
BILLS
YOU LEFT THE BROKEN SHARDS OF OUR MAGIC GENIE LAMP IN THE DRIVEWAY, DANY! IT WAS THE FIRST THING I SAW WHEN I CAME HOME!
WHOOPS.
YELL YELL YELL
YOU NEED TO RESPECT OUR BELONGINGS--
WHO KNOWS WHAT THE HINN WILL DO ON ITS OWN--
YELL YELL YELL YELL

DID YOU WISH TO BE SKINNY, MOM?
...
LINDA! OF ALL THE THINGS TO WISH FOR!
LOOK, MADISON, WHEN YOU'VE WALKED A MILE IN MY SHOES—
LINDA DOESN'T HAVE TO EXPLAIN HERSELF TO YOU!
AND YOU WISHED FOR A GUITAR AND A LUCKY LOTTO TICKET?
GUITAR—? I STARTED PLAYING FOR STRESS MANAGEMENT. AND THAT LOTTO TICKET IS PROVIDING FOR—
HONEY, REMIND ME TO CALL THE COMPANY, THERE'S SOMETHING WRONG WITH THE PAPERWORK AGAIN—
DANIELLE RADLEY, YOU ARE GROUNDED.
GIVE ME YOUR LAPTOP-- YOUR PHONE--
I WANT YOU COMING STRAIGHT HOME FROM SCHOOL--
NO FUN--!!
WHAAT?! FOR HOW LONG?
A MONTH!
CAN'T I KEEP MY PHONE FOR EMERGENCIES?
nod
OKAY, BUT YOU REALLY ARE GROUNDED, YOU KNOW.

...AND NO MAGIC.
GIVE US WHATEVER MAGICAL DOODADS YOU'VE BEEN HIDING FROM US.
BUT--
NO BUTS.
...
HIDE
UNIVERSAL REMOTE

FINE! HERE'S MY MAGIC REMOTE CONTROL AND MYSTICAL INSECT REPELLANT RING.
THAT'S ALL THE MAGIC I HAVE.
Universal REMOTE
REALLY?
I SWEAR ON THE HOLY BIBLE.
...
...I DIDN'T TAKE ANYTHING FROM ELMA'S, REMEMBER?
GOOD. THANK YOU, SWEETIE. I DON'T WANT YOU MESSING AROUND WITH MAGIC AND GETTING HURT.
BUT WE ARE GOING TO HAVE TO TALK ABOUT THIS.
A LOT.
nooooooooo

WHO'S GOING TO CATCH THE DOG, THEN?
WHAT?
I WAS JUST WONDERING WHO WAS GOING TO CATCH THE DOG IF DANY CAN'T LEAVE THE HOUSE.
ARE YOU TELLING ME WHAT TO DO?!
Shhh
DO YOU THINK ANIMAL CONTROL CAN HANDLE A GENIE?
AND EVEN IF SOMEHOW THEY COULD-- COULDN'T THEY TRACE THIS HINN BACK TO YOU?
YOU'RE RIGHT. DANY, YOU LOST THE DOG, YOU HAVE TO FIND IT.
I UNDERSTAND.
YOU'RE STILL EXTREMELY GROUNDED! GO TO YOUR ROOM! WE'RE GONNA TALK LATER. I'M VERY DISAPPOINTED.
MADISON, HONEY, YOU NEED A RIDE HOME?
OKAY!
TRUDGE

SIGHHHH...
...WHERE'S CLONEY?
...NICE AND **CONVENIENT** THAT SHE **MISSED** THIS WHOLE DISASTROUS SCENE.
MOTO PSYCHO
SUMMER S
CUPS
CINEMA
Car Bros XXIII This time it's impersonal
MR. GREAT GUY 2 THE SUMMER SOLDIER
POXAR presents CUPS
I wanna be a plate!
NO
Ding!
GOOD GRADES
Be Best
Ding!
A Super Family
6:13
MADISON:
We have a dog genie on the loose Meet in the woods at 7 to discuss
LEAH:
wHaT????? also im supposed to have dinner with my family?
TOM:
!!!!

tee hee
...Here she is now!!
...Double Dany...?
smek
Pikki...?
I TELL YOU, THIS IS HOW PEOPLE SHOULD LIVE.
hm...
IN A LITTLE PIKKIBALL? SEEMS A BIT LONELY.
WHIRRR
whinny!

Chef Penny Sez: Enjoy Your "SPAGHETTI"
IT'S FINE! EVERYTHING'S FINE!
CHECK THIS OUT!
spaghetti?
why did you–?
SPLETT
ew.
SINK
NO RULES!
WHERE DOES IT GO?
I dunno!
I CAN'T EVEN MESS UP THIS PLACE IF I TRY. IT'S LIKE I TYPED IN THE CHEAT CODE OF LIFE. MY ROSEBUD.
FLOP
I USED THE CHEAT CODE OF LIFE IN THE SINS: HOUSE PARTY AND IT MADE THE WHOLE GAME POINTLESS.

IT'S LIKE A TIME-SHARE, LEAH! BUT INSTEAD OF A CONDO IN FLORIDA, YOU SHARE... MY TERRIBLE LIFE!
unconvinced
...AND JUST LOOK AT THAT BATHROOM!
HOW IS THIS POSSIBLE?
THIS BATHROOM IS SICK!
WE'RE IN OUTER SPACE?! WHOA!
WHAT HAPPENS IF THE GLASS BREAKS?
THE VAST ABYSS WOULD CONSUME US ALL.
WOW

MINAKO
LILITH
SHE'S HOW MY SOLAR POWER MANIFESTED! HER NAME IS BUDJAWUDJA. I TAUGHT HER TO SHRINK.
...BUDJAWUDJA?
KISS
IT'S BECAUSE SHE'S A **CUTE WITTLE BUDJAWUDJA!!**
BUDJAWUDJA, SHRINK!
BEEM
AWW!
snif
HEHE, THAT TICKLES!

I CAN'T BELIEVE YOU SNUCK OUT THE NIGHT YOUR PARENTS GROUNDED YOU!
Shameless!
IT WAS MADISON'S IDEA!!
MAG
HEY, DANY SQUARED LOST A DOG GENIE, AND I THOUGHT IT SOUNDED LIKE A JOB FOR THE SOLAR GEEKS.
WOO! A SOLAR MISSION!
THE LONGER THE DOG GENIE IS LOOSE, THE MORE DANGER EVERYONE IN MELTON IS IN!
WE CAN SET UP PATROLS, DO RESEARCH ON--
HEY! LOOK!
"HINN. THE ETERNAL COMPANION AND SERVANT TO AN UPPER ECHELON OF DEITIES, THIS TYPE OF DJINN APPEARS AS A FAITHFUL DOG."
Dieties PLURAL??
DOOM DOOM
ALERT:
MOM!!
NO! GUH! INITIALIZE CONTROLS!

eject
INT. BEDROOM
WE MADE A HOLOGRAM THAT PRETENDS TO DO HOMEWORK.
...IT WAS HER IDEA.
HONEY?
h-hi, Mom!
H-HI, MOM! JUST DOING MY HOMEWORK.
SORRY TO INTERRUPT.

YOU KNOW, I CAN'T HELP FEELING LIKE A HYPOCRITE.
THERE I AM, YELLING AT YOU FOR PLAYING WITH A MAGIC REMOTE CONTROL AND A CITRONELLA RING. WHEN I'VE DONE SO MUCH WORSE.
I DIDN'T KNOW-- WHEN I RUBBED THAT MAGIC LAMP--
I MEAN, I RUBBED IT WITH A LYSOIL WIPE. I DIDN'T KNOW IT WAS MAGIC. I DIDN'T UNDERSTAND THE CONSEQUENCES.
...THAT DOG IS NOT GOOD AT GRANTING WISHES.
DANIELLE, HONEY, I DON'T WANT YOU FALLING INTO THE SAME TRAP. YOU HAVE TO BE BETTER THAN ME.
WH-WHAT'S WRONG WITH YOUR WISH?

EVERYTHING TASTES TERRIBLE; IT FEELS LIKE A CURSE.
I GOT WHAT I ALWAYS WANTED. BUT I'M... CURSED. I CAN'T BE HAPPY.
AND DAD...
WE JUST DIDN'T KNOW WHAT WE WERE SIGNING UP FOR.
...I DON'T WANT YOU TO HAVE TO GO THROUGH THAT.
YOU HAVE ALL THE TIME IN THE WORLD AHEAD OF YOU FOR MESSINESS.
ANGEL AMELIA
SOMETIMES I WISH YOU AND LAUREN COULD STAY LITTLE FOREVER AND NEVER HAVE TO DEAL WITH--
hehe
YOU BETTER NOT HAVE SAID THAT TO THE DOG GENIE!
HOLO-DOLLY

ha ha
I DIDN'T.
REACH
FLINCH!
hurt
HAIRY POTTER
...
SORRY. SOMEDAY YOU'LL UNDERSTAND.

YOU LIE TO YOUR PARENTS *SO EASILY...*
MOM...
I THINK I REALLY HURT MY MOM'S FEELINGS.
Aww... cloney...
LINDA'S TOUGH. SHE CAN HANDLE IT.
SHE--
SHE WOULD'VE PUT HER HAND THROUGH THE HOLOGRAM... IF I DIDN'T...
SIGH
copying to "Mom"
MOM
exit
PLAN.doc
PATROLS:
Cloney & Dany daily
① Joan & Leah (Mon.)
② Madison & Aleesha (Wed)
③ Dany/Cloney(?) & Tom (Thurs.)
31

welcome
SHADY MEN
FSHHH
PFTH!
SMOOSH
SHADY MEN
census Bureau
GROW
rummage
HAND MY PARENTS THESE MEMORY-SOFTENING T-SHIRTS. THEY SHOULD MAKE ME UNGROUNDED.
AND UNHURT MOM'S FEELINGS.

I LOVE
daught
census Bureau
DISSIPATE
woman, you're my woman....
SOY
BILL
BILL
Past Due
CREDIT APPLICATION DENIED
hi.....

WELCOME HOME, SWEETHEART.
I THOUGHT YOU WERE IN YOUR ROOM.
THE FAULT IN OUR KIDS
JUAN VERDE
I LOVE MY DAUGHTER
I, UH... HUH?
blink blink
YOU'RE SUPPOSED TO BE **GROUNDED!**
WHY? DANY'S BEEN SO GOOD!
my daughter
CHUCK? ARE YOU--
I LOVE MY DAUGHTER.
I LOVE my daughter

DANY! WHAT DID YOU DO?!!
I ♥ MY DAUGHTER
HOW DID YOU EVEN DO THIS?!
DID YOU--
DID YOU CATCH THE HINN?
N-NO... I...
I USED MAGIC!!!
PARENTAL DISAPPOINTMENT
...I CAN'T BELIEVE YOU'D BE SO DECEITFUL!
YOU LIED TO MY FACE!
AND IF I HADN'T BEEN WEARING MY PROTECTION AMULET--
WHAT DID SHE DO?
no no noOOOOOO wake up Dany
I DON'T KNOW, CHUCK, SOME SORT OF SPELL?
MOM, I-- I'M SORRY--

YOU'RE SORRY YOU GOT **CAUGHT.**
DOESN'T THAT COUNT?
HOW DID I **BELIEVE** YOU WHEN YOU SAID THAT WAS ALL THE MAGIC YOU HAD?
I LOVE my daughter
OH MY GOD! IT WAS RIGHT THERE IN FRONT OF US--
THE GRAPHIC MEMOIR, CHUCK!
H-HOW DO YOU KNOW ABOUT--
I FOUND IT IN YOUR WASTEBASKET. IT WAS JUST SITTING THERE!
DAD AND I THOUGHT IT WAS CUTE. I WAS SO PROUD OF YOUR CREATIVITY.
I LOVE my daughter
SO OUTLANDISH, I NEVER EVEN THOUGHT IT COULD BE TRUE.
WHEN REALLY, IT WAS A CONFESSION.
--!
STOMP
STOMP
STOMP-
POOR MADISON... SO SHE'S YOUR...
...IMAGINARY FRIEND...?
FLIP
She's a real person!!
(did you even read it?!)

...WHERE IS IT?
FLIP FLIP
...THE SKETCHBOOK?
SPRINT!
SLAM

A LOCK THAT WILL ONLY--
WHAT ARE YOU--!
BAM
AHHH!!!
I ♥ my daug
roll
YANK
HOLO
happiness
POOF
CLONK
I LOVE my da
HOLO

yell
yell
MOM... PLEASE... DON'T USE THE SKETCHBOOK.
...
I WON'T. I PROMISE.
OKAY.
HOW CAN I TRUST YOU AGAIN?
BZZT!
I THOUGHT SHE'D **NEVER** SHUT UP.
snif...
I'VE LEARNED MY LESSON.
GET REALLY, REALLY GOOD AT HIDING OUR TRACKS.
I MEAN, DOES SHE REALLY EXPECT US TO **LISTEN** TO HER? SO NAIVE.
2 MATH
emergency
AN EXACT REPLICA OF MY MAGIC SKETCHBOOK, WITH THE MAGIC INTACT.
IN YOUR **FACE**, MOM!

RUMBLE
RUMBLE
DOOM
KRRRR
WUH-WHAT DID WE DO?!
LIMITLESS ROLL OF UNIVERSAL REPAIR TAPE! **PLEASE** TELL ME THIS NEW SKETCHBOOK WORKS!
KRRRR
IT'S-- IT'S NOT WORKING--
shake shake
KRRR

IT'S GETTING WORSE--!
KRRR...
rumble rumble rumble
By the rays of the sun, TRANSFORM!
SOLAR HEALING POWER!
HEY, HELP ME OUT!
FWOOO
B-By the rays of the sun TRANSFORM!
SOLAR HEALING POWER!!!

IT'S WORKING!
wiiu
wiiu
...HEAR SOMETHING, CHUCK?
YEAH.
Guh...
wheew

POP
huff huff
JIGGLE JIGGLE
SOLAR FLARE!!
wuh-where do-

FZZZZ
CHKK
DID YOU HEAR THAT?!
HEAR WHAT?
I HEARD A LOUD SOUND-- I **FELT** IT.
...I DUNNO. MAYBE THE CIACCIOS' TREE FINALLY FELL.
badump badump
OH.
YOU KNOW THAT IT'S WRONG TO MIND-CONTROL, DON'T YOU, DANY?
YEAH.
IT SCARES ME THAT YOU'D EVEN TRY.
I-- I'M SORRY.
I NEED TO BE ABLE TO TRUST YOU.

Lenny's GARDEN MOVERS
"A little to the left"
BANK
YOU LOOK SO GREAT, LINDA.
FRUIT PLATE
ELMA
C'MERE, ADELE.

UNHH! I LOVE IT WHEN MOM COOKS! REMINDS ME OF THE GOOD OLD DAYS.
REMEMBER HOW MOM USED TO MAKE THAT MAYO SALMON CASSEROLE, EVERY YEAR ON MY BIRTHDAY? SHE SAYS SHE'LL--
HA! GOOD DAYS. WITH DAD?
YOU EXAGGERATE, DAVE. DAD'S JUST STRICT. AND--
--AND KEEP IT DOWN. SOME OF US DON'T BURN EVERY BRIDGE WE CROSS.
YEAH, DAVE. YOU DON'T GET TO CHOOSE FAMILY.
HMPH.
WINO FOREVER
ACCUSE
YOU HARDLY ATE, LINDA! AT LEAST HAVE SOME PIE?
I'M GOOD. LOOKS DELICIOUS, THOUGH.
IT IS DELICIOUS! I MADE IT!
DIET ZOLA
YOU LOOK GREAT ALREADY, LINDA. YOU DON'T WANT TO TAKE YOUR DIET TOO FAR...
IN A BIT, TRACY.
DID I TELL YOU-- CHARLIE WON'T EAT CAKE ANYMORE! HE DOESN'T LIKE IT! CAN YOU BELIEVE IT?
WHAT AN ADVANCED PALATE, RIGHT?

SUSAN AND I JUST GOT A CALL FROM MRS. CORMANSKI. SHE SAYS CHARLIE MIGHT HAVE TO SKIP A GRADE OR TWO.
WOW.
THEY FINALLY NOTICED—
—WHAT A SMART ONE THIS IS. CHIP OFF THE OLD BLOCK.
PAT PAT
... He doesn't love me.
SQUIRM
OH, DAVE, CONGRATS ON THE BREAKTHROUGH. SUSAN WAS JUST TELLING ME—
THEY'VE NEVER SEEN ANYTHING LIKE IT. WE'VE GOT GOVERNMENT CONTRACTORS SNIFFING AROUND MY WORK AT THE LAB.
slide
...SO THEY FINALLY OFFERED ME TENURE. MASTERSON TOLD ME THEY WOULDN'T, BUT HE'S EATING HIS WORDS NOW.
NARESZCIE. BETTER LATE THAN NEVER.
I NEVER HEAR OF A PROFESSOR GETTING TENURE AFTER SO LONG DEFERRED—
IT'S NOT THAT UNCOMMON! YOU DON'T KNOW WHAT YOU'RE TALKING ABOUT, DAD.

...WHOLE FAMILY OF LOST CAUSES.
Thanks, Grandpa...
SEEMS LIKE WE'RE ALL FINALLY FIGURING THINGS OUT.
DAVE WITH THE LAB...
LINDA WITH YOUR DIET, AND CHUCK WITH HIS CASH4LYFE, AND ME WITH THIS RECORD REAL ESTATE BOOM!
(YOU CAN BENEFIT FROM THE BOOM TOO, IF YOU WANT MY HELP!)
CASH TODAY!
FREE APPRAISAL!
10%
CALL AUNT TRACY NOW!!! (203) 555-1789
IT'S AS IF THINGS ARE FINALLY COMING TOGETHER FOR ALL OF US. THE WAY IT'S ALWAYS MEANT TO HAVE BEEN.
CHEERS TO THAT!
CLINK
CLINK
heh
WHAT'S SO FUNNY, TRACE?

Paris
Baguette
NOTHING, NOTHING.
After you...
CAN I OFFER YOU A SODA, DANIELLE?
ER... SURE.
YOU WANNA GOODIE?
DO YOU LOVE CHEESE?
Yip!
YOU DO!
CHOMP CHOMP
BabyTab™
NEWS LOCAL
vandalized, Could it be the Blue Bandit?
KILLER CLOWN STILL ON THE LOOSE, UNREPENTANT—
School emergency funding falls

Store vandalized: Could it be the BLUE BANDIT?
NEW
Blue Bandit fan concept art
Dusty's Old-Fashioned Vacuum Warehouse was vandalized last night, its entire inventory of vacuum leaners destroyed beyond repair, d a mysterious blur locals have bed The Blue Bandit, captured ecurity footage, is the only lead estigators so far.
YOU'VE NOTICED IT TOO? SOMETHING'S NOT RIGHT IN MELTON.
huh?
JUMP
Is Baby Tab spying on your
Yes.
MISSING PERSONS REPORTS SPIKE IN MELTON, CT
was it something I said?
Real Estate
Weath
MELTON PET STORE ROBBED
REGISTER UNTOUCHED
You've reached your free article limit. SUBSCRIBE?
BLUE BANDI
MELT
VACUUM WAREHOUSE VANDALIZED
BLUEBANDITWATCH.com
BLUE BANDIT: URBAN LEGEND OR PUBLIC MENACE?
POLL:
urban legend
Evidence?
BabyTab™
SCROLL SCROLL
Dusty's OLD FASHIONED VACUUM WAREHOUS
11:40
WANTED
NO DUMPLINGS
cuuute...
you're gonna get rabies
nuk?

LOCAL NEWS
SPEEDING TICKET ISSUED
TOP 10 BLUE BANDIT FAN THEORIES...
SHOVE
NICK MALONEY! THAT'S **MY** LOCKER! WHAT ARE YOU DOING?!
NOTH--
YOU'VE BEEN LEAVING ME THOSE **SECRET ADMIRER NOTES?!**

I SAVED YOU! YOU WERE A PIG! AND THIS--
A PIG?
DO YOU REALLY NEED TO RUIN MY LIFE?! WHY NOT TAKE A DAY OFF?
HUH?
NICK LIKES THAT GIRL?
?
HAH! SHE THOUGHT I ACTUALLY HAD A CRUSH ON HER.
oh
BUT IT WAS ALL JUST A PRANK.
...harsh
WHY WOULD YOU MESS WITH SOMEONE'S HEAD LIKE THAT?
YOU'RE AN EASY TARGET.
OOOOOOHH
OMG DRAMAAA
OOOHHHH
FIGHT! FIGHT!
I CAN DESTROY YOU A THOUSAND DIFFERENT WAYS. BUT I WON'T.
ohhh!!

BUT JUST KNOW THIS.
NO MATTER WHAT, I'LL NEVER FORGET.
UNTIL I'M OLD AND GRAY.
THE FIRES OF MY **HATRED** WILL BURN YOUR NAME **FOREVER!**
CRACKLE
DOES LOCKER GIRL LOVE NICK?
WHAT? NO! DO YOU UNDERSTAND **WORDS?**
I **HATE** HIM! TIMES A MILLION!
WELL, I HATE YOU RIGHT BACK!
LOCKER GIRL IS GOING CRAZY!
ha ha
ohhh
I'M NOT CRAZY!!!
yikes

...I SHOULD'VE KNOWN IT WAS YOU WHEN I SAW THE AWFUL SPELLING AND CLICHÉD IMAGERY.
Ohhh
CLONEY!
ARE YOU OKAY?
I SOLVED THE MYSTERY OF THE SECRET ADMIRER NOTES. IT WAS...
NICK MALONEY.
AW, HONEY...
Shut.
YOU WANT ME TO BEAT HIM UP FOR YOU?
CHOCO
SIGH. NAH.
I'M SO READY FOR REAL DANY TO GET CABIN FEVER IN HER PIKKIBALL AND DECIDE TO LIVE HER OWN LIFE.
HINT, HINT.
UHH, I'M GOOD...
(SOME THOUGHTS ON WIGGING OUT IN THE HALLWAY, THOUGH...)
Sup Real Dany

HEY, CAN I BORROW YOUR FLYING RING FOR A FEW DAYS?
YOU LOSE YOURS?
I'M ALWAYS LOSING MINE; I HAVE LIKE THREE AT HOME.
HEY, GUYS.
KEEP IT!
YESTERDAY WAS MADISON'S AND MY DAY TO PATROL FOR THE HINN--
THE BLUE BANDIT!
IT DOES SEEM PRETTY LIKELY THEY'RE ONE AND THE SAME.
I WANTED TO SEE THE PUPPY AGAIN...
YEAH, THERE WAS NOTHING GOING ON.
AND I WAS THINKING... THE HINN MIGHT NOT **WANT** US TO FIND IT.
IF WE COULD ONLY **MAKE** IT WANT... OOH, RICE CRUNCHIES!
DARK CHOCO

...ALEESHA STILL WANTED US TO "HELP THE WORLD" OR WHATEVER, SO SHE FOUND US SOME UNDERPRIVILEGED KIDS TO TUTOR.
MAGIC IS REAL!
REACH for the CLOUDS!!
so if you fall you stay on the ground
Library Hours:
YAY
"Aliens walk among us" Abe Lincoln
Phonics system invented by Blaise Pascal
I FOUND A LEAD ONLINE, THOUGH. SUPPOSEDLY MAGICAL DOG COLLAR. IT'S FIFTEEN THOUSAND DOLLARS ON UPPERSTRATA.
OOH!
BUY IT!!
PREMIUM PRICES
CIRCUS
SHOULD WE SPLIT UP? MIGHT GO FASTER.
STRESSÉE MOI? OUI!
COMMERCIAL SPACE FOR RENT
IRQUE
CIRQUE de SUBURBIA
NO REFUNDS

ha
ha
ha
?! ha
ha
ha
ha
I BET YOU CAN'T GO HIGHER THAN ME!
IN YOUR DREAMS!

SKYE JOHNSON
FRIDAY
ELECTIVE ART 7-3
face
CLOUD MONET
PAINT
PAPER
TIME!
LET'S HEAR IT FOR KATIE; GREAT JOB MODELING.
JUST-- TRY NOT TO MOVE AROUND SO MUCH, OKAY?
WHO'S NEXT?
yeah
tap tap
ART
ANY VOLUNTEERS?
SHRINK
NICK, WHY DON'T YOU GIVE MODELING A TRY?
That's a first
SNICKER
STAND
SNICKER
SK8R BOI
heh

MRS. JOHNSON, I CAN'T SEE HIM FROM HERE. CAN I MOVE TO A DIFFERENT SPOT?
THERE'S AN EMPTY CHAIR UP HERE.
DUDE. THE BACK OF HIS HEAD IS SQUARE.
YOU'RE RIGHT. HUH. THAT REALLY HELPS ME DRAW HIM.
I'M UGLY
heh heh
HEY, WHY IS YOUR HEAD A SQUARE?
...
snicker snicker

interesting....
FLIP
ha
ha
YIKES
...Goblin Boy...
ha ha Ken stop
TIME! OKAY, WHO'S NEXT?
glance

YOU READY TO FLY AROUND AIMLESSLY LOOKING FOR THE **BLUE BANDIT**?
YUP.
MELTON'S VERY OWN CRYPTID. MY LIFE IS AWESOME.
SPORTS
MAYBE WE CAN LOOK FOR THE HINN **AND** VILLAINY AT THE SAME TIME? NO ONE'S HAD ANY LUCK ON PATROL YET.
STOP
31
YEAH! I'M READY FOR WHATEVER LIFE THROWS AT ME!
CHECK OUT WHAT I CAN DO.

wobble
wobble
YOU BEEN WORKING ON THAT TRICK?
yeah!
SKITTER
AAHHH!! KILL IT!
LEAVE HIM ALONE. HE'S JUST A FELLOW TRAVELER.
Look at him go!!

HAVE YOU SEEN THIS DOG?
HAVE YOU SEEN ME?
THE BLUE BANDIT? I WISH...
DANG, JONAS, THIS FRISBEE IS SITTIN' TIGHT.
whoa
WOW
LET US KNOW IF ANY CRIME NEEDS TO BE FOUGHT!
PLEASE TAKE A FLYER!
LOCAL HEROES
HAVE YOU SEEN ME?
TIPS? CALL
EXCUSE ME, MA'AM—HAVE YOU SEEN THIS DOG?
SHOO! GO AWAY!
...
mrow
hiss
Yay Kitty!
here you go!
SOLAR FLARE!
THAT'S NOT GONNA BURN THE KITTEN, IS IT...?
WHAT DO YOU THINK I AM, A SERIAL KILLER?
UHH... THIS ISN'T OUR CAT...

THERE'S NO HINN AND NO CRIME TO FIGHT. MELTON SUCKS.
WE DID SAVE ALL THOSE CATS.
Don't even look at them...
weirdos, Mommy!
MAYBE WE SHOULD GO BACK TO SPOTS WHERE THE BLUE BANDIT WAS SPOTTED. LIKE THE VACUUM STORE.
BUT I ALREADY LOOKED THERE!
YEAH, BUT HE MIGHT'VE LEFT A CLUE YOU MISSED.
OOH! WAIT!
DELI
IT'S A NEGOTIATING TACTIC. DOGS LOVE CHEESE.
ALSO I'M GETTING HUNGRY.
BOTTLE SUGAR JUST ADD WATER!
FIRE WOOD
ENTER
CHEESE
ATM
SOFT SERVE ME!
ERMAGHERF!
PARKING FOR Dusty's OLD-FASHIONED VACUUM WAREHOUSE ONLY
AW... POOR PUP'S HUNGRY...
THE BLUE BANDIT!

G'BOY! COME HERE!
YOU WANT CHEESE?
WAFT
Sniff
YOU WANT CHEESE?!
RUFF!
Yes!
AWW! WHAT A SMART DOG!
SIT!
Pet
COULD USE SOME TRAINING.
...PLEASE TELL ME I PACKED THE LAMP CLONEY MADE...
OKAY, GOOD BOY. GET BACK IN THE BOTTLE.
SO YOU'RE REAL DANY?
sniff
pet pet
YEAH. CLONEY WEARS A PONYTAIL. SHE CALLS IT HER CLONEYTAIL.

OKAY, BABY, GET IN THE BOTTLE.
scratch scratch
AXEL!
RUFF!
My human summons me.
NICK?
SQUINT
WHAT ARE YOU DOING TO MY **DOG?!**
IT'S NOT JUST A **DOG!** IT'S A HINN, A DOG GENIE--
--IT'S THE **BLUE BANDIT!**

I KNOW WHAT AXEL IS. AXEL, C'MERE, BOYYYY.
POOF
RUFF.
POOF
What shall I do with them, master?
WE'RE TAKING THE DOG!
HE'S **MY** DOG.
AND, YEAH, I LEARNED ABOUT THE **WISHES.**
JUST WAIT. YOU'LL SEE.
SHEESH. NOW WE **REALLY** HAVE TO TAKE THE BLUE BANDIT.
YEAH. YOU ARE **LITERALLY** THE **WORST** PERSON TO HAVE MAGIC, NICK. AT LEAST TOM AND I ARE TRYING TO BE **SUPERHEROES.**
YOU'RE MORE OF THE **SUPERVILLAIN** TYPE.

SORRY, BUDDY.
Dusty's OLD FASHIONED VACUUM WAREHOUSE
DON'T CALL ME "BUDDY." YOU'RE NOT MY BUDDY.
NICKY? DID YOU INVITE YOUR FRIENDS OVER TO PLAY?
NO, **MOM!** GO BACK INSIDE!
OKAY, NICKY.
TURN

"NICKY"?
LEAVE ME ALONE!!
FWOOSH
CLOSED UNTIL FURTHER NOTICE
FWOOSH
FWOOSH
LUKE GET WELL SOON!
MELTON BEARS
ha ha loser!
STUPID DOG! THAT WASN'T WHAT I MEANT!
Dusty's
FOR SALE
NO DUMP

?!
WOOOSH
NEED AN ESCAPE?
Come dine at VESUVIO'S in Scenic
CAUTION: HOT
GARBAGE FIRE INC.

TOM?
coff coff
HELP??
TOOOOMM!!
SOLAR FLARE!!
CAUTION: HOT

Solar Flare!!
cough cough
FLING!
?!
TUG
cough cough
BAM!!
ARK KNIGHT OF THE SWOLE
Winner of Several AWARDS!
The New Jersey experience
NJ TP
PATH
& other fine ways of exiting NJ

COUGH
COUGH
COUGH
COUGH
COUGH
COUGH
NEED AN ESCAPE
COUGH COUGH... ARE YOU... COUGH?
I'M SO TIRES
cough
cough
cough
NEED AN
Magic Phone, where are we?
NEED AN ESCAPE?
VISIT OUR KIOSK AT NEWARK AIRPORT
TRY IT TODAY!
You are in Newark, New Jersey.
GETTING SUED? GOOD
WE NEED TO GET THE HINN BACK FROM NICK. EVERY MINUTE HE HAS--
wheeze
wheeze
COUGH COUGH
TURN
WE'LL FIGURE SOMETHING OUT.
PAT PAT
KOFF

WHAT IF YOU DRAW A MAGIC-DAMPENING FORCE FIELD GENERATOR?
ENJOY RESPONSIBILITY
SPONGES
CHIPS
TWIGS n STIX
GET THAT PUPPY INTO A FORCE FIELD AND—
MY MOM TOOK MY SKETCHBOOK AWAY.
Hydrogen Fortified Water
...SHE PROMISED NOT TO USE IT...
IS YOUR MOM **TRUSTWORTHY?**
UH...
XL Lemon Chamomile Cheltzer
SHE COULD TEAR THE **FABRIC** OF **REALITY!** WHY ARE YOU JUST MENTIONING THIS NOW?!
WELCOME TO SKEEZY MART
PLEASE WASH YOUR HANDS
FREE AIR
PUSH
KORN DOG
S-SORRY!
UH...
sorry gimme a sec
DOO DOO
Skeezy Mart
MAMA?
NO, I'M FINE. GONNA BE HOME LATE.
YEAH, WITHOUT ME. OKAY.
LOVE YOU TOO. BYE.
SK
GULP
Lemon Chamomile

FOR RENT
MEDICAL OFFICE
MEDICAL LICENSE
MEDICINE
CALL xxx-xxxx
SKEEZY MART
Vesuvio's II FINE DINING
MOBSTERS EAT FREE!
WE'VE GOTTA TELL EVERYONE ABOUT NICK, AND THE HINN, AND THE SKETCHBOOK--
...SO I THINK MOM'S MAGIC AMULET PROTECTED HER FROM MY MAGICAL MINDWIPE T-SHIRT, AND ONCE SHE REALIZED WHAT I TRIED TO DO--
A T-SHIRT?
NO ONE CAN RESIST FREE T-SHIRTS. I WAS TRYING TO GET UNGROUNDED.
I **ALWAYS** WONDERED WHY THE SCHOOL GAVE OUT T-SHIRTS COMMEMORATING A **LIFE-THREATENING METEOR STRIKE.**
IT WAS **YOU** WHO MINDWIPED EVERYONE AFTER THE GYM ATTACK.
??
...
IS THAT WHY EVERYONE THOUGHT IT WAS A METEOR?
BUT IF WE REMEMBER PRINCE NEPTUNE, DOESN'T THAT MEAN WE WEREN'T MINDWIPED?
DANY...

DANY WOULDN'T MINDWIPE US!
...JUST LOOK AT YOUR SHIRT, JOAN!
I SURVIVED MELTON METEOR
WHY WOULD YOU BRAINWASH YOUR FRIENDS?
Y-YOU WOULDN'T LISTEN TO ME... IT WAS ALL I COULD THINK OF...
SHAME
SHAME
whyyy
boo hoo...
SO, WHAT'S THE BIG NEWS?
EVERYONE'S MAD AT ME; GO PRETEND TO BE ME AND APOLOGIZE TO THEM...
...
DANY, YOU'RE NOT FOOLING US!
I'M SORRY. I'LL NEVER DO IT AGAIN, I SWEAR.
emerge

YOU COULD JUST MINDWIPE US AGAIN AND MAKE US FORGET THIS.
ohh...
whisper
WHEN I SAW HOW NICK TREATED HIS MOM-- I DON'T WANT TO BE LIKE HIM. EVER.
UM, SPEAKING OF NICK: HE MAY HAVE THE BLUE BANDIT, BUT I'VE GOT SOMETHING...
IT'S MADE OF DJINN BLOCKS. IT'S SUPPOSED TO HAVE A HANDICAP EFFECT ON MAGIC. I GOT IT ON THE INTERNET.
WOW!
COOL!
IT'S WORTH A SHOT.
...AND THEN KATHLEEN INVITED ME TO THIRSTY THURSDAY. I WAS IN SHOCK.
...SITTING WITH THE COOL KIDS... HAHAHA
...TOOK LONG ENOUGH...
...if Gene could see you now...
STAHHP!
hi

WHY DO YOU SMELL LIKE SMOKE?! DO WE NEED TO HAVE A "TALK"?
I SWEAR TO GOD, MOM, I WAS JUST ADJACENT TO A PILLAR OF BLACK SMOKE. THAT'S ALL.
sniff...
TRACE'S HELPING US FIGURE OUT THE PAPERWORK FOR THIS CASH4LYFE MESS.
...SHE SAID IT'S ILLEGAL TO TAX US BEFORE WE'VE COLLECTED OUR WINNINGS.
HI, HONEY! LINDA, TELL HER THE NEWS.
I GOT A PROMOTION AT WORK.
THEY PUT ME ON THE HENDERSON PROJECT.
How2.com
DECLARING BANKRUPTCY
WOW, CONGRATS, MOM!
welcome home
IT'S GETTING LATE— LET'S FINISH THIS TOMORROW, OKAY?
WHAT IF WE MOVED AWAY AND STARTED OVER SOMEWHERE ELSE? WOULDN'T THAT BE FUN?

HONEY. CHANGING YOUR EXTERIOR CIRCUMSTANCES WON'T CHANGE THE PROBLEMS INSIDE. TRUST ME ON THIS ONE.
THERE'S A SCHOOL DANCE COMING UP. IT'S GONNA BE REALLY LAME AND IN THE SCHOOL PARKING LOT. WE'LL PROBABLY ALL GET RUN OVER BY DRUNK DRIVERS. CAN I GO?
THAT'S FINE WITH ME.
R-REALLY?
I MEAN... I DON'T MIND STAYING HOME.
I KNOW.
SO YOU... WANT ME TO GO TO THE DANCE?
I NEED TO GO TO THE MALL, ANYWAY. I'LL HELP YOU PICK OUT YOUR DRESS.
THE DANCE IS TOMORROW.
WHY DIDN'T YOU TELL ME SOONER?
sigh

BECAUSE I DON'T WANT TO GO? MADISON IS MAKING ME.
I SKIPPED ALL MY SCHOOL DANCES. EVEN PROM.
AND I REGRETTED IT LATER. I DON'T WANT THAT TO HAPPEN TO YOU.
YOU'LL HAVE FUN. I PROMISE.
...
...NOW GO TAKE A BATH.
2:10 pm
6m ago
MADISON:
DANY!!! Come to the
I'm dying!!!!
1:45
MADISON sent you a reminder: "DANCE 2NITE!!"
ALERT: Sad memes for you!
hm...

ha
ha
ha
Decorations
ha ha
...
SAVE ME
CHEER
THIS WOULD BE A LOT EASIER IF WE COULD FLY.
HAND ME MORE STREAMERS.

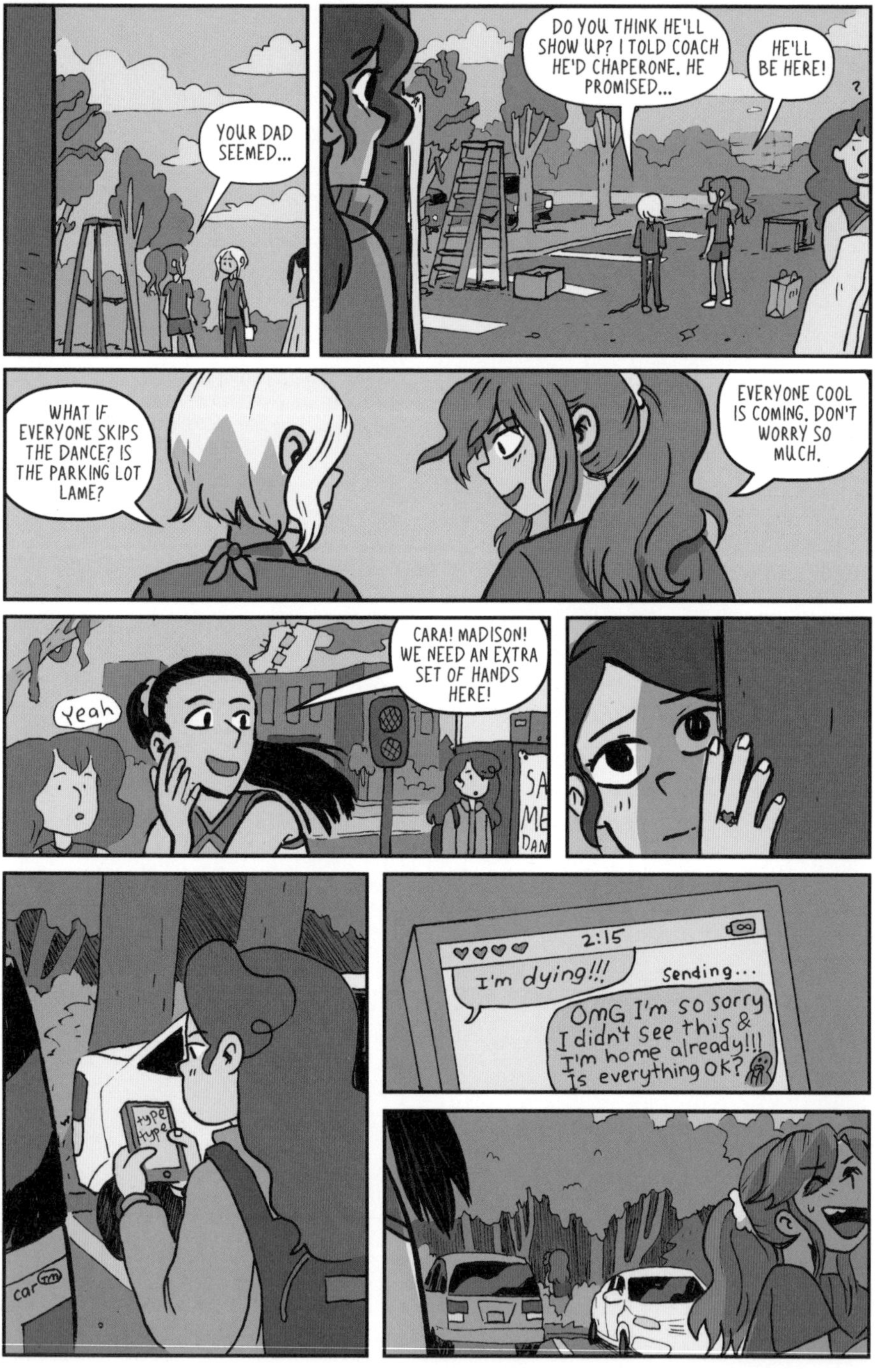
YOUR DAD SEEMED...
DO YOU THINK HE'LL SHOW UP? I TOLD COACH HE'D CHAPERONE. HE PROMISED...
HE'LL BE HERE!
?
WHAT IF EVERYONE SKIPS THE DANCE? IS THE PARKING LOT LAME?
EVERYONE COOL IS COMING. DON'T WORRY SO MUCH.
CARA! MADISON! WE NEED AN EXTRA SET OF HANDS HERE!
Yeah
type type
car™
2:15
I'm dying!!!
Sending...
OmG I'm so sorry I didn't see this & I'm home already!!! Is everything OK?

I CAN'T DO THIS.
C'MON, DANY! YOU'RE GOING TO HAVE FUN.
I DON'T EVEN WANT TO GO! I'D RATHER WATCH.
YOU'RE BETTER AT LIVING MY LIFE THAN I AM, ANYWAY.
BZZZZT
WELL, YOU'RE NOT GONNA GET ANY BETTER AT IT BY LYING IN BED ALL DAY.
YOU DON'T KNOW THAT FOR SURE...
CLÖN LABS

LOOK, I'M NOT INTERESTED IN BEING YOUR SUBSTITUTE DANY FOREVER.
I HAVE ASPIRATIONS OF MY OWN, YOU KNOW?
I WANNA HIT THE ROAD, JOIN THE CIRCUS, AND LIKE, GO ON SOME CRAZY ADVENTURE.
BECAUSE I'VE GOT NO PAPER TRAIL! I CAN BE ANYONE!
NO ONE WILL LOOK FOR ME! CAN YOU IMAGINE?
WHILE YOU'RE STUCK IN SCHOOL, I CAN BE BUSKING ON STREET CORNERS WITH MY RAGTAG GROUP OF CIRCUS FRIENDS...
...YOU WANT TO LEAVE?
well...

I PROMISE YOU, NO MATTER WHAT, I'LL STICK AROUND UNTIL WE'VE BECOME THE COOLEST--
ER, A MODERATELY ACCEPTED INDIVIDUAL.
CLÖN LABS
SO I'LL GO TO THE DANCE. I'LL TRY TO WIN OVER ALL THE RANDOS FOR YOU. DON'T WORRY.
BUT YES. SOMEDAY, I'LL HOP A FREIGHT TRAIN OUT OF THIS PLACE.
SOMEDAY.

WANT ME TO DROP YOU OFF RIGHT HERE?
OKAY.
HOW DO I LOOK?
CURTSY
BEAUTIFUL.
SO BEAUTIFUL I HAVE TO DOCUMENT IT.
DROP OFF
Cheeee...
CHIK
YOUR HAIR, DID YOU DO SOMETHING TO IT?
MOOMM!!
USUALLY IT HAS SO MUCH VOLUME--
FLUFF FLUFF
Bat
Bat
I STRAIGHTENED IT!
WHERE'S MADISON? I WANTED TO GET PICTURES OF YOU TWO TOGETHER.
hurr hurr hurr

I THINK WE'RE DOING PICS INSIDE AT THE DANCE.
AW...
hang on...
...WANT ME TO TAKE ONE OF THE TWO OF YOU TOGETHER?
OH! UH...
OLDER SISTER, RIGHT? NO WAY YOU'RE **HER** MOM.
NO THANKS, I'M *FINE*.

SUIT YOURSELF.
CALL KENNETH.
LINDA RADLEY?! IS THAT YOU?
DENISE?
OH MY GOD!
YOU LOOK SO THIN! YOU LOOK FANTASTIC!
WHAT IS YOUR SECRET?
CONGRATULATIONS!
Oh haha I'm a monster right now. This is the LAST ONE.
ha
ha

...I DON'T KNOW IF I EMAILED YOU ABOUT THIS ALREADY, BUT SOME OTHER MOMS AND I STARTED A MOMMY BOOK CLUB. DOES THAT SOUND LIKE SOMETHING YOU'D BE INTERESTED IN? ARE YOU STILL A BIG READER?
I'VE BEEN MEANING TO JOIN A BOOK CLUB FOR THE LONGEST TIME!
bye!
WAVE
one of my kids is an HONOR RO STUDENT
LAST MONTH WE READ **WHY MEN LOVE SPORTS,** AND THIS MONTH WE'RE READING **THE SEVEN-SECOND DIET.** ARE YOU AROUND THURSDAYS?
This way to SAVE MELTON
SAVE MELTON DANCEATHON!
GOAL:
WE DID IT!
$3000
$600,000
PAY HERE
SAVE MELTON DANCEA

I gotta feeling (woohoo)
...that we're all gonna have a good good time...
DANY!!! you made it!!
...hoping for an uneventful liifeee party party feeling riight

ooh baby I love parfaits, every day
THE 8th GRADERZ
WOW... EIGHTH GRADE IS GONNA BE SO COOL.
Katrina is the KEWLEST
I WANNA START A BAND.
ME TOO.
I USED TO KNOW THE VIOLIN.
I CAN ALMOST PLAY THE UKULELE.
DIBS ON DRUMS!
I HAD A DREAM ONCE WHERE I PLAYED THE BASS.
A PROPHECY?
WATCH OUT, CARNEGIE HALL.
MAYBE WE CAN BE A VERY OBOE-CENTRIC BAND.
...THEY'RE NOT EVEN HOLDING THEIR INSTRUMENTS RIGHT. GOD!

DON'T CALL ME BACK UNTIL YOU'VE GOT SOME GOOD NEWS! I'M AT MY DAUGHTER'S-- YEAH-- FIX IT!
TURN
EUGENE. EUGENE MCCOY.
ARE YOU CARA'S FATHER?
YOU KNOW MY GIRL?
...CARA'S JUST **WONDERFUL.**
SHE'S GOOD FRIENDS WITH OUR MADISON.

MADISON! MADISON'S A REAL SPITFIRE. SHE'S GREAT.
HOLD ON, I GOTTA TAKE THIS--
TALK TO ME, KENNETH...
The Blue Bandit?
Dude...
4SALE: Choco LAST CHANCE 50 cents
PAY HERE
IS THAT NICK MALONEY?
THE MEAN KID? IS HE HERE? WHAT DOES HE LOOK LIKE?
...HE'S GOT MAGIC, LEAH! HE MADE HIMSELF... DIFFERENT...
HE NORMALLY LOOKS LIKE AN EVIL LITTLE TROLL. THAT'S HIM OVER THERE.
where?
TIPPYTOE
HIM?!
YEAH.
whisper whisper
LITTLE NICKY IS A BULLY?!

HUH? YOU **KNOW** HIM?
YES, A LITTLE. HE GOES TO MY CHURCH.
YOU CALL HIM "LITTLE NICKY"?!
heh heh
THAT'S WHAT **EVERYONE** CALLS HIM. I DIDN'T EVEN KNOW HE **HAD** A LAST NAME.
THOUGH I GUESS HE'S... BIG NICKY NOW...
creepy...
BRB
I CAN'T BELIEVE **LITTLE NICKY** IS YOUR BULLY.
GUYS!
I JUST SAW NICK MALONEY! HE BROUGHT THE BLUE BANDIT!

YOU! KATIE! ASK ME TO DANCE WITH YOU.
NICK, WOULD YOU... DO ME THE IMMENSE HONOR...
NO.
MY LIFE IS A LIE!!
NEXT!
DANCE WITH ME, NICK! PLEASE!
are you okay?!
??
SELL!
CHOCO
nom nom
YOU'RE UGLY. GO AWAY, SARAHLEE.
PAY HERE
FRESH DIPPY

CARA. YOU'RE IN LOVE WITH ME. ASK ME TO DANCE.
ew
boo hoo
Uh...
NICK! I'M DESPERATELY IN LOVE WITH YOU! DANCE WITH ME!
?
how-?
CARA!
LEAVE HER ALONE!
OH, LOOK. IT'S THE **SOLAR GEEKS**.

WHAT... JUST...
YOU'LL PAY--
MADISON. GO CLIMB A TREE.
YOU THINK YOU'RE **POWERFUL.** YOU'RE **NOTHING** NEXT TO DANY.
NEXT TO **ALL** OF US.
heh
IF YOU'RE SO POWERFUL, WHY DON'T YOU COME DOWN FROM THE TREE?
LEAVE HER ALONE!

DANIEL THE MANIEL. ASK ME TO DANCE.
GRRR...
murph murph murph.
I DIDN'T CATCH THAT.
Hance... Hith...
CLENCH
DANCE WITH ME!
NICK... YOU CAN'T... DO THIS...
YES I CAN. I CAN DO WHATEVER I **DREAM.**
sneak

... YOUR... DREAMS ARE STUPID...
WANT ME TO TELL AXEL TO REMOVE YOUR MOUTH?
YOU KNOW WHAT YOU ARE? YOU'RE NOTHING WITHOUT YOUR MAGIC.
AM I WRONG? AXEL, LET'S SEE HOW SHE DOES WITHOUT HER MAGIC.
!
FWOO
FWOOF

CLONEY?!!
D-DANY?
Maiden China
MACHINE WASH COLD
I—
I DIDN'T
MEAN—

ALERT! ALERT!
ALRIGHT ALREADY!!
EMERGE
GASP
ALERT: Pikkimal Life-Form TERMINATED
N-no!!! CLONEY!!!
THIS CAN'T BE HAPPENING...
CLÖN LABS
EXIT
BZZT
BRING HER BACK!
HOW DID YOU--
UNDO IT! PLEASE!
I... I DON'T KNOW HOW...
STUPID DOG...

BY THE RAYS OF THE SUN, **TRANSFORM!**
TRANSFORM
POSE!
FIVE AGAINST ONE? TCH, **THAT'S** FAIR!
AXEL, COME **HERE!** WHAT ARE YOU DOING?!
JOAN— THE COLLAR! TAKE IT!
you didn't mean it...
huff huff
ruf?

SPITE
OW!
...MAKE THAT SIX AGAINST ONE!
YEAH!
GET HIM!

BOO
STOP IT!!
ANGRY MOB 101
STOP IT!!!
RAFFLE
SPLOOSH

C'MON, WHAT THE HECK?!
SORRY...
UGH! THIS WASN'T SUPPOSED TO HAPPEN! AXEL!
USB
COME HERE! WHY AREN'T YOU LISTENING?
GET AWAY FROM THEM! STUPID DOG!!
GASP
KICK
GOT IT! THE COLLAR'S WORKING!
CLICK
YELP!!

AXEL!! COME BACK!!
mrow?
BARK
8th graderz
ON
EATHON
BARK
BARK!!
MEOWLP MEE...
AHHHH!!

MEEOW
MEOWW
MEOWWW
nyan nyan nyan nyan
mew mew mew mew
MEOWWW
MEEOW
chkchkchkchk
THE 8th
MEOW MEOW MEOW MEOW MEOW MEOW MEOW MEOW MEOW MEOW
MEOW
BARK
mew mew
HE'S NOT LISTENING TO ME ANYMORE--
OOWWWW MEOOOOW
AAHHH
BARK
TELL MCSALLY I WON'T NEGOTIATE!

...THEN WHY ARE WE PAYING HIM? SORRY, KENNETH, I CAN'T HEAR A THING YOU'RE--
DAD!
BARK
SOLAR FLARE!!
CREEK CREEK CREEK
YANK
CHOMP
NGH!
RUFF

FWOOO
O
DAD?
CREE
CREEK
chkchkchk
AXEL, CALM DOWN. THE COLLAR'S GONE.
Bruff
YOU'RE GONNA BE GOOD, RIGHT?
AXEL, I NEED TO BE STRONG. BIG AND STRONG AND POWERFUL, OKAY?
LICK

GROWTH SPURT
HAH! YOU'RE LIKE A LITTLE DOLL.
YOU'RE **ALL** SO LITTLE. HEH.
WHAT'S SO WRONG WITH BEING LITTLE?
IT MEANS YOU'RE WEAK! AND I'M STRONG!
BUDJAWUDJA! I SUMMON YOU!

LITTLE NICKY!
D-DON'T CALL ME THAT! WHY ARE YOU HERE?
DUH, I GO TO THIS SCHOOL TOO!
LITTLE NICKY, THIS **ISN'T** VERY **CHRISTIAN** OF YOU!
I DON'T CARE!
WA HHH
BRUSH
OW!

HEY BULLY BOY!
scoff.
I DON'T LIKE YOU.
AND I LIKE EVERYONE!!
TRUTH BOMB
... the truth hurts.
PUPPY KICKER

YOU'RE WRONG! THAT'S NOT WHO I AM! NOT AT ALL!
SOLAR PUNCH! x4
!!
PRY
Phew!

TAKE A LOOK AT WHAT YOU'RE DOING, NICK.
WHAT ARE YOU GONNA DO ABOUT IT? YOU'RE NO MATCH FOR ME.
MAYBE YOU'RE RIGHT.
BUT DO WE REALLY HAVE TO FIGHT? MAYBE WE SHOULD JUST TAKE A STEP BACK AND...
meow
munch munch
WHAT'S YOUR REAL NAME, BABY? IS IT REALLY AXEL?
wag

I have gone by many names... Axel is just one of them.
WOOF
But in my old life, my happiest times, I was known as... Penelope.
Throughout the ages, one thing has remained constant—
this quenchless, ravaging hunger—
YOU POOR THING!
DO YOU LIKE CHOCOLATE, PENELOPE?
Bruf?
CHOCO
RUFF.
Yes.

EVERYONE, LOOK! SHE LIKES CHOCOLATE! AWW!
ISN'T CHOCOLATE POISON FOR DOGS?
AXEL! NO!! DROP IT!
hnn...
PENELOPE?
Hnnk! Hnnk!

SQUAK
hack hack
AXEL?!
WHAT'S HAPPENING?! MAKE IT STOP!!

HYUGHHHh
MORF
THE MAGIC IS WEARING OFF!!
MORF
Get me SPREADSHEET KENNETH
MORF
mew
SAVE MEL

MORF
I WANTED TO BE A CAT
MORF
hiss
DAD! YOU'RE OKAY!!
MORF
SPREADSHEET OF ALL THE BIRD FEEDERS IN TOWN—
—and...cancel that, *COUGH* the situation just changed...

PUPPY!
I'm sorry
Pet
PENELOPE! YOUR COAT-- IT CHANGED! ARE YOU OKAY?!
RUFF.
SO CHOCOLATE IS BAD FOR DOGS...?
I GUESS I'VE NEVER REALLY... **HAD** A DOG BEFORE.
BABY...
YOU'RE SO FRAGILE!
Kiss
EW, JOAN! SHE JUST PUKED EVERYWHERE!
mrow
SAVE MELTON!
AXEL...

JUST TAKE YOUR DOG AND **GO.**
...THAT'S NOT GOING TO HAPPEN.
MRS. MARKS!
YOU, DANY?
I DON'T EVEN **KNOW** WHAT TO DO WITH YOU.
MAGIC IS REAL?
I'LL TALK TO YOU **LATER.**
BUT **YOU,** NICK?
YOU'RE **SUSPENDED INDEFINITELY.** WE'RE GOING TO HAVE A CHAT IN MY OFFICE. COME WITH ME.
I SUGGEST YOU FIND THE DOG ANOTHER HOME.
I'LL TAKE HER! **DIBS!**

AM I A MAN WHO DREAMED I WAS A SQUIRREL?
OR AM I A SQUIRREL WHO DREAMS I AM A MAN?
REX? SKYE? ...CAN WE KEEP HER?
MADISON...
PLEASE, BE REALISTIC.
PLEASE?
PLEEEEASE?
REX AND I HAVE OUR HANDS FULL WITH YOU KIDS! WE CAN'T JUST ADOPT A MAGICAL DOG!
BUT... MAYBE... WE CAN TALK ABOUT ADOPTING A NICE STRAY FROM THE POUND.

...BUT WHERE WILL PENELOPE GO?
I'LL TAKE HER. IT'S MY MESS TO CLEAN UP.
SEE?
...
C'MON, PUP!
MAGIC IS REAL!! MY LIFE IS A LIE!!!
WHOAAOOH
8th
raderz
do you believe in magic? In a young dog's bark
...I'LL BE RIGHT BACK.

MAGIC IS REAL, MAGIC IS REAL, SING IT WITH ME!
MAGIC IS REAL, MAGIC IS REAL...
FOONP
MI
Tees
MAGIC IS REAL, MAGIC IS REAL...
I danced my CARES AWAY at the SAVE MELTON DANCEATHON
ARE THOSE FREE T-SHIRTS? NICE!
HEY!!
WHOA...
SOLAR FLARE!
HEY! NOT COOL!
FSHHH

TRUST ME, YOU DO **NOT** WANT THESE T-SHIRTS.
I DID...
FSHH!
my stick!
cough MAGIC IS REAL cough cough
UNPLUG
sheesh...
SAVE ME
Ooooh...
CLAP
CHAOS ARPEGGIATING!
LAAAAAAAAA
SHRED
BADUMM
PERFECT PITCH
WOOOO!
Phew

HMM...
FLAP FLAP
...I GUESS I **COULD** FIX THE SCHOOL MYSELF.
THERE'S JUST ENOUGH POWDER TO DO THE JOB.
LEAVE IT! NOT FOOD!
SNIF SNIF
SHAKE

GROW!!
COULD YOU REPAIR THE ROOF OF THE GYM?
NOD
grrr...
...SCHNOORR...
THERE YOU ARE! OH, GOOD, YOU HAVE PENELOPE!
WHATCHA DOING ALL THE WAY OUT HERE?

I THOUGHT SHE COULD USE SOME PEACE AND QUIET.
rub rub
SO...
...ARE YOU GONNA BRING BACK CLONEY?
...I CAN'T.
SHE SHOULDN'T HAVE EXISTED IN THE FIRST PLACE. BUT ALSO–
I'D BRING YOU BACK IF ANYTHING HAPPENED TO YOU.
WELL, NOTHING'S GONNA HAPPEN TO ME! SHEESH.
WHAT ARE YOU GONNA DO WITH PENELOPE?

I DUNNO. SHE'S JUST A NORMAL DOG NOW, SO--
ARE YOU GONNA... GET RID OF HER?
WHAT? **NO!**
I WAS JUST GONNA **SAY,** SHE'S NO LONGER A THREAT TO THE GENERAL PUBLIC.
I DON'T KNOW WHERE TO PUT HER, THOUGH.
ha ha
MAYBE I CAN STILL CONVINCE REX AND SKYE! SHE COULD BE MY EMOTIONAL SUPPORT DOG.
pet pet
OR WE JUST GIVE THEM SOME NICE MINDWIPE T-SHIRTS?
I DESTROYED MY BAG OF T-SHIRTS.
MADISON, IT'S NOT A GOOD PATH TO GO DOWN.
BUT--!
SHE CAN LIVE IN HERE!
THE PIKKIBALL!
TILT
DOG MODE

DOG MODE
UPDATING......
type type
YOU'RE SAYING I CAN KEEP THE PIKKIBALL?
WELL, IT'S PERFECT FOR PENELOPE.
AND WITH... CLONEY GONE...
...IT'S LIKE SHE NEVER EXISTED.
I NEVER WANTED TO HURT ANYONE AT ALL. YOU KNOW THAT, RIGHT, MADISON?

OF COURSE I DO.
LET'S GET BACK TO THE DANCE.
BUT I'M NOT READY...
THE PARTY'S NOT GONNA WAIT FOR YOU!
EXIT

CMON! you'll have fun!
CHEER!
I DON'T CARE WHAT I SAID BEFORE! I TAKE IT BACK.
autographs
YOU'RE COOL IN MY BOOK, DANY.
WOO!
MAGIC IS REAL!
...
ReAlly?
DANCEYDANCE
YOU SAVED MY DAD'S LIFE. YEAH, DORK.
YOU'RE COOL NOW.
pat pat
Cloney... we did it...

WOW... I'M... COOL NOW.
congrats?
WELL, YOU'RE NOT HIDING WHO YOU ARE ANYMORE! PEOPLE HAVE THE CHANCE TO KNOW THE REAL YOU!
MAGIC IS REAL
WOOO!
MAGIC IS REAL, MAGIC IS REAL
Be my friend!
BUT MADISON! WHAT IF THEY ONLY LIKE ME BECAUSE OF MY MAGIC?
DOOMM
...JUST TAKE THE WIN, DANY!

Dany's back!
WAVE
PARTY
SOLAR FLAIR!
THE END!

it's PENELOPE'S PUPPY COMICS CORNER!
Ruff.
Here is a selection of my earthly adventures.
I CAME BACK EVENTUALLY
ALL RIGHT, PENELOPE, BACK IN YOUR BALL.
PIKKIBALL, GO!
!!
TOSS
SCAMPER
PENELOPE! NO!
DOG IS MY CAR PILOT
I WISH TO BE THE COOLEST BOY AT THE DANCE!
FWOO
FWOOSH
BUT I'M NOT 16! WHO'S GOING TO DRIVE--
Ruff.
!!
Get in.

PAW-TROLLING THE STREETS

PENELOPE SAYS:

Follow your dreams!

KRISTEN GUDSNUK

is the creator of MAKING FRIENDS, an IndieBound bestseller, as well as the Henchgirl comic series. She was born in suburbia, didn't go to art school, and now lives in Queens, New York, with her boyfriend and dog.